# The Dihedrons Gazelle-Dihedrals Zoom

LESLIE SCALAPINO

The Post-Apollo Press
Sausalito, California

ISBN 978-0942996-72-2


LIBRARY OF CONGRESS CATALOGING-IN-PUBLICATION DATA
Scalapino, Leslie.
The dihedrons gazelle-dihedrals zoom / Leslie Scalapino.
p. cm.
ISBN 978-0-942996-72-2
1. Prose poems, American. I. Title.
PS3569.C25D54 2010
811'.54—dc22 2010018455
Cover art: Jess Collins. *Hera Closing With Herakles,* 1960. Collage, 19.5 x 23.5 inches. Courtesy Tibor de Nagy Gallery, NY. © The Jess Collins Trust.
Cover and book design: Amy Evans McClure. Typeset in Sabon.

The Post-Apollo Press
35 Marie Street
Sausalito, California 94965
www.postapollopress.com

*Printed in the United States of America on acid-free paper.*

*For Tom always, with love*

*And in memory of my mother, Dee Scalapino*

# Author's Note

Dihedrons and Gazelle-Dihedrals are human-like creatures. Profoundly injured, they roam jetting space in the form of vertical severed halves. *The Dihedrons Gazelle-Dihedrals Zoom* was written by leafing through *Random House Webster's Unabridged Dictionary* choosing words by process of alexia, not as mental disorder but word-blindness: trance-like stream overriding meaning, choice, and inhibition. The intention to bring about an unknown future was changed by this action of alexia making as it happens sensual exquisite corpses—leading to the discovery that there *isn't* any future, isn't even any present. Such an exquisite corpse, read, is in an instant yet not even in 'a present.' Outside's events unite gluing to each other a single object. That which had already existed is by chance. Dysaphia: as if the people can have no sensations, the writing becomes the sensations that are then felt by everything.

The exquisite corpses are physical as if one such is flesh-butterfly-other-occurrences (real-time events such as the exploding of Mumbai), each event-cluster internally hybrid rather than being separate presentation as idea. That is, the writing is not the idea of the whole framework of occurrences after without its existence ever being.

*That which had already existed is by chance*: not only includes events in real-time but visual scenes existing before the writing was created—Jess's collages, Kiki Smith's prints, a painting by Masami Teraoka. These are not illustrations of the writing, nor are they the inspirations or the subjects of the writing; rather, the visual images were later (after writing) linked to passages of text that show the same reality, in discovered composite actions (in the case of Jess's collages), thus seen in the outside. Teraoka's painting of an octopus sucking a woman's front is linked to the same event in the text; a *memory* of *his* image was simultaneous at the instant of writing the first passage that has this image: seeing our memories making the present.

A single petal parts the whole/air terror in one/ga•ril´•a(s) killing in a spree at the cricket meet the boy ga•ril´•a lying sleeping on the car motor gore that came from him as it pulls into the fleeing crowd is dead. There he is. Eidetic empty eidos 2 flowering both the sight [and] that of its own interior concept are empty at once. Actions halved are not assembled or dismantled each time whole the petal in outside flows.

## The Contester

The contester reaches the red chela into the streaming crowd cheliform extracting the dark blue poppies. Walking, *one* saw a dark blue poppy [and] [seen] one night. The 2 trembling part. Day begins anywhere. A forest on many stems rushes a single tree on stem. *One* had realized the small boys kidnapped, sold to later wait on the kidnappers (parents, when they're old), [the boys] are slaves too—as are the orphan girls (girls are defined as "those not killed," the word "girl" erased for others); they'd rather kill all______ [girls/hands motions are dactylology] and kidnap and enslave all boys than change. The family ocker (redundant) doesn't even remember—or doesn't remember at all (two entirely different events). But memory isn't the origin of events. Neither is. The eye is (*not*). Oar. The hand thrust in. The red claw, the mitt reaching the poppies some red-centered, has performed actions, though the action is the contester's, already past but appearing at once 'allowing' the single petal outside not producing or attached in wind—outside isn't either, the trees fractionators future only, a forest 2 states a tree rushes 1000 trees roiling divided are in that sense 2 frothing the appendages bats bat the sky corners of the diamond [in which the base runner runs] floats in the sky where a forest as single entity bats blows—the sky. Yet petal exudes dawn there exactly. Not even gradually 4 there is *no* memory. If there were not a contester the dark blue indigo-plum black-purple-centered poppies are for nothing? Fractionators wings flock trees bulk on stems the whole a musical instrument a stem an appendage as the base runner moving is on appendages hearing is the parts of these or the poppies from the current.

# Cheliform

'The flew' (the girls who flew and their action that being past is single/singular) the girls who lifting off flew/disperse pink frocks in the hyperbaric weight too he poles the onlookers of the parade with the red chela mitt [it] poles where being within the crowd's rim extracts the dark blue poppies extraction is once he moves on their lining. The contester chordate coming to the crowd lining the street as horses go by as a man would whose jaw making sores in his oxygenless flesh his irradiated blood vessels having vanished swim breathing the pure oxygen in the diving bell there. Thus submerged swimming oxygen in the diving bell breathing infuses his jaw with oxygen from which new blood vessels grow as small girls in pink dresses fly before the perambulator disperse and flap across the street dissilient in pink flashes to flock behind bushes further on emerging shout in surprise at the pusher a mother far from the contester a man being before the crowd that is facing 'their'/the crowd's parade—so the contester is inside (their) mid (inner) side line, inside the crowd's lining, is between in their midst but alone standing outside them also his head outside the crowd his arm in the red mitt chela claw when pacing lion-like/lioncel eyes lidless yet he's extending exposing the cephalochordate palm red-segmented lenticule reaches into the not even wavering stalwart standing crowd, their and his choreutics action from amidst *them*, and with the chela extracts the bunched black-centered dark blue purple poppies. Memory *is* here (at once as they occur) the origin of the events but in their middles.

# [the children think invisible]

of the ga•ril´•a a boy slipping in the gore on the motor itself motionless as car moving he/now it lies on the engine dead in the crowd of the dead and living injured of the cricket team when attacked by terrorists as the flow flowers huge pulling in asterism amidst or in them the sides-dihedron (planes as sides of open people) flaps in one (is) intestine-jewel-coil liver-heart of one having opened each is ‘an’ side *seen*. As if for him the universe were a steady state in which nothing happens, except extraordinary, rather than huge waves or small waves passing through on it sometimes a huge wave the economy one such passing over it may overturn a person—a man on the board of a charity won’t give money if the emergency is related to the economy 4 he sees it as outside (*not*). Sees it as affecting everyone therefore *not* real (emergency)? That wood be only a trees falling on *one*? The attack on the cricket team guerillas ga•ril´•a(s) by killing policemen guarding the players and cricketers are killed wounded but replaced (the event is replaced) by the Han crowd killing in a rampage through the Uighurs’ factory dorm a venography like warrens the rabbit/the pacesetter of the base runner however assigned conchoid plane as equal stable space in which actions are/will be, the base runner’s venogram of his interior in ochre marking on him. The rudderpost of the brawl the Uighur factory workers being beaten the latter post ruddle heaped Uighur corpses images on the internet that are then suppressed censored seen. The rabbit *that is pacesetter* for the base runner apparent to him suddenly, for the game’s form controlled by them—?—means it’s/the game’s a lie. Band expanded stretching he runs between ever extended bases or waits on one brinksmanship Asteroidean an avatar star starfish is speaking for everyone as the children careening arm-in-arm in bubble flickers billboards replace the first avatar grinning Cheshire had the blushing star in the air monitors (the starfish replaces the Cheshire cat’s head grinning speaking in the air in *Alice* the monitor here embedded motionless in sky except blinking in the streaming falling asteroids) [the children think invisible are not speaking therefore? there the events replaced in their minds, *they're* the events? A man scoffs snickering at the side "those people can't know" since they're girls its voice projected implanted seeming to be there in whatever circumstance floating] embedded in context. Embus people to the games [speaks]. Oar people lying in inner tubes on the lake. Hear at dark the heart's lake. Alleyoop cries the [monitor] the basketball player far away while another one nearer stuffs the ball into the high basket of the court at dusk traversed light by the feet of players seeming arc-back to flow in the reverse direction.

# Ebullient

a be ce dar i um. Not an abacist. The question had not been answered how the orphaned girls (only motions in the place of the word the not-dead), thus slaves from shortly after birth (rather than killed by parents abandoned raised in orphanages the one founded yet to later conceive breed, to be workers, future prostitutes), could learn to read? Their flashing of messages reading in the air with their hands was a dactylology invented by them, the girls, and passed on wild-fire. But from books? It's plants [silent] hearing from birds never, who sing so they're together. In the space between. *Rather than* [their being there—they are] rather than are *with* the dainty fast white Arctic dog's feet moving when she/the wolf-whitedog dreams running.

# Meadow of dissociative disorder

Certain joy gemma in the outside in one [allowed] at hearing the people coasting surfing after the Iranian election was rigged usurped they're posting on Twitter coordinate times of protest marches servers closed down find Twitter-feeds servers outside their country communion is conchoid plane conciliar an equal space/plane of the actions Uighurs being sealed in their city by the Han lipemia whose military now kills the Uighurs. A man saying the Han are calming them. Though posting outwardly Uighurs after some murdered injured by the Han mob after their hearing a rumor whipped up of the Uighurs having raped a Han [the Hans] brawl rampaging through [Uighurs'] factory dorms buggerall the conchoid plane is equal space of action not stemming from conchoidal made by a blow, only slightly later than coordination on Twitter of protesting the election the Han mob running through a Uighurs' factory dorm "brawl" really rampage murder in the conchoid equal space corridors of action outside the Uighur workers who photographing the heaped conchoidal/torn corpses post the images on Twitter march peacefully having their servers closed the Uighur city sealed are killed inside the action the city a venogram ochre markings ruddle painted on the Uighur dead flaps as if of plants open on the small children's heads the soft ductile seen in the purple light to hear everywhere there's only seeing others see. Statocyst the sacs' equilibrium indicate position in space of the Asteroidean avatar server spread starfish floating mound with legs in a meadow of dissociative disorder internet and phenomenal yet as intentional temporary alteration in identity monitor speaks to the base runner the man when he runs by, now. Above the people's parade lining the street stars move appear seemed implanted substituted for anyone to be able to speak in the midst of the star legend the enlarged diamond whose bases the base runner not only has to/*has* run but find here. When the Asteroidean star encountered by the base runner—a star as Cheshire's head floating starfish in the city when the base runner comes to the lake to drink, his/the base runner's heart's lake has a tie to this outer lake—assembling the Asteroidean infusing sky and internet green meadow of dissociative disorder at once center red star blushing indigo substitutes for Cheshire cat sign grinning in the city air space though through streets the horizon has buildings on it when *Asteroidean* star whose head (—is then? red Chrysanthemum was/ is smiling mouth with teeth barely visible in its red middle petals yet that appear there Mongolian wrathful deity red one is in the sky above the street speaking the dead everywhere around them the Chrysanthemum cars rose blown caught in the crossfire of soldiers and citizens who now rise fighting the bombers knowing finally "they're just *killers*" citizens née insurgents borne in it everyone immediately turns away hearing this burst put their hands over their ears until one stops,) moves on. But some of the children either the Lost or abandoned the kidnapped do that action erased children who are still small halve the air as action of walking even. Events *will be*—as (merely/and) *just replaced* that instant. Everything visions in them passing through the sides 'forward' phenomenal [as if they/ as sights *weren't*—phenomena—for them *to be*].

# Float

Out of which the silent dactylology from emerald wastes little girls crossing the roads arriving the green meadows full they do the cakewalk and are celebrated with cakes for their most intricate steps. Either reinventing or reading. Those arriving cakewalk everywhere others having perished or escaping locked dorms for the workers in mines and factories live in camps by cities edges. Some live in trees by the stream of girls stretched lying on the limbs at night girls pull plums from the trees "Give them to us" the Secretary had said ("rather than kill them," was her meaning), announcing the opening of a single orphanage the first to be for the millions the female infants and children killed each year so obviously there's overflow of the dazzling white streak small white wolfdog wolfwhitedog streamer-aura of them in the sky above floats. Outside the one orphanage mothers with caked breast having turned them in the other little girls are harnessed and given dog-tags, those not in the orphanage who are on floats through the streets. Have the dog-tags. The little white wolfdog Distaffer's avatar is that of many children who play the shape of it left in the air as their (each child's) shape is left there many are above the rose horizon Venus is resting red and brown crisp curled huge flowing leaves millions deterge by Venus resting that fallen from trees hurl vomiting the blue sky of the car flowing toward the leaves (flying that vomit the car's blue sky coming hurtling to them) through the coursing flow of red-brown leaves a man skateboards crossing toward/and the skateboarder is *before* the windshield of the car's flow overflow elation at brim or rim without horizon color or sides. The powder monkey jockey finds the orphan living with her in a tree before she's lost again. To each other the floats move slowly parade yet the white wolfdog streaks playing at once each as briefly each shape has a manifestation in the rose and

blue. Little wolfwhitedog having learned this like variation like touchless
4 blue weather is dysaphia. without senses

*(top)*

# Soft Green

The notion of their being as young in its openness that all the while distich contained ending only in one alive at the same time seeing in them their reactionary being curtailing the Collective—none—the reactionary through distichous bright green leaves sees from the perspective of the eternal child. 'Then' becomes the subject of the other's hate, no more than everyone.

# Soft Green

The soft green meadows composed new blades of grass that rose. That rose grew in the midst of the baby blue sky growing from the meadow a bugout walking night then midst the meadow by the time a drone shoots over operated from outside soldier on its way to kill some people on the road they're conjectured as terrorists by evidence not yet heard or assembled yet the cattle in the meadow's swatch of floating black they are that, are in blackness as crowd and not evening or light while sky there undulant fever all the cattle passing as by line-of-sight looking at each other but no contagium other than their being alive there pass contagious abortion between them and begin to spontaneously abort the slick forms. The bugout doesn't produce. Everything does? Is the katabatic wind that flowing downhill coming from the meadow of soft green—inferior vision in a dream reading, a man correcting oneself dreamer a woman reading as luminous green words appear—so the reader has to consider himself to be a woman fetuses of the cattle floating before their eyes part of them so that knitted to them permanently as disseminating in the wind in blades of grass the fetuses snagged beside them. Theogony, cattle not dictating ever hear and turn in the wind. A Dicktest named for G. F. Dick who devised it was for scarlet fever though, useless to them. The daughter the deb having learned to spit out others become Artemis is in hard joyous bounding a gentle deer kite by her side going into the war-torn regions. The reader who'd had the dream in green had been a brownie for only a short time when a little girl, but the only photo of her in her brownie uniform the bugout had not run retreated from combat or been in it yet is now permanently bound to the cabbagy fetuses of cattle as kites oar machine drones in a sort of dielectric at once a dielectric loss similar to—and the woman *as* it—the butterfly blood-reef (Chrysanthemum dyslogia), wrath deity/Chrysanthemum does not see that she is separate from the butterfly blood-reef—ever, at any time.

## Deterge character

The butterfly blood-reef had been—is—the woman encased in the whirring red chrysanthemum in being it can never be peeled away or pried out of her or from it for it is her is death-fan the purple forest creating limbs outside and plants doing so—dysphoria, she's by being opposite of creating—its pair at once. Isn't a dream though eminent rather fact emittance of her character—where there is no fate except people's character, a person's fate is their character emission nebula already in place? no, one resists this—no one, a sort of delay screen phosphorescent one does not deterge as or senses causal/while delay has the same effect. The horse rearing also is the petaline red Chrysanthemum whirring emergent for an instant. Insides coincide. Insects the emerald green crickets at night sing before the tramontana wind.

# The

The Distaffer had come down gently (the plane) in the black flowers in black beds landing the plane lightly where all around lines of the orphan girls the main industry migrating coming up through holes of the underground petroleum and lines of them crossing the vast black beds could/can be seen. She had deposited her cargo/she deposits her cargo then, undetected by the scouts the jets.

# The

Straying from her route in cloud beds the time she's detected by the jets come close almost touching her flying plane flying above and below two zoom as a pair fire on her plane. The time over the ocean she sinks coming in the legs the center that hump of the avatar pink octopus spreads onto her sucking her middle the pudendum the girls separate slowly swim beside fins in the ocean. The fins glide beside them sunlight glancing off of the fins everywhere the lines of swimming girls go forward unseen from above in the sun [unseen by the jets their/jets and girls on the surface almost touching and blinded by it] giving her head air lying on the bed of sunlit waves the hump like cephalate on her front coming the jets go over blind as they're reflected in the glints of waves.

# Plane

Man ruffled in wind and motion of his back seeming to be flying forward of blown back (away) ascending blackened backlit in halo of the illumined high sun it is seen it's his front moving forward ruffling descending to light on the ground angelic. WHOK! of the ball from him slamming as he lights on the court again. Birds speaking come to one where zooms the small white wolf-dog in the air comes up. One first dreamed petting it now is. So it's back wards and illumined.

## The Distaffer's memory

one of working on a hill, paid less than minimum wage by an employer who shouted at her crashing her spirit yet the part voided (in the memory) of wading amidst flowers plants leaves on the hill at the end of the day her clothes covered with dirt she walks down the hills home. Walking down the hills goes through the streets one leafy avenue being fraternity-sorority row where the debutant sorority girls are in rush and throw open a door clapping forming a bower of clapping under which the recruits the rushees pour out to the street and meet the Distaffer clothes and face covered with dirt (earlier on the hill she'd wept, touching her face with dirt on her hands) who meets them inadvertently mingling their flooding onto the sidewalk as she goes through them the deb is among them who are clapping singing to recruit in the rush they narrow their eyes disapprovingly seeing the young woman outside walking on the row. Who is dirty. She'd conjectured they saw her as a bum. But that there occurred only an instant of seeing, if that. In fact, this is *not* a memory of the deb's, who has never seen the Distaffer. For the deb the event [of the row] not occurring they meet. And the Distaffer remembers this flood always every time of going on the row that part of descending the hill the event circulating as a happy memory in her from the part voided though present of first wading in flowers? in marvel of descending the hill seeing wading through wild beings clapping rushing narrowing their eyes.

# The katabatic wind

A/the katabatic wind flowing forward downward on it floats a slope of night the city flowing beneath as a lit band flicking is detached at a different time from the first thunder heard in a fresh night. Thunder-rattle occurs after in warm summer's night breath. At day line of little girls go on the sidewalk buoyed upright by each holding floating a balloon—the line of balloons floats them on strings. Their forward is sideways seen from by in outside. To obliterate the seeing of such images any becomes a man's purpose yet only those actions occurring as the onlooker noticing *their* sights (of these actions, the action's sight) as being at-once-with-their-actions but the actions that are or are of the sights wildly blind outside—have no designation—can only be blind to be on or go down a slope of night? There is space yet is only in one's experience at night's delative reverse-out. 'Then' delaminates. But as in undertow she doesn't turn violence back. The thick-necked black horse its neck bowed anyway into the katabatic wind plants its feet the horse on the long legs swaying as it's plunging on the slope blind then because it's black the night is can't ever come to the base of the slope the night can't.

# The Dactyl

The eye edges crenellated as the small eye of elephant weak at the keyhole is Cheney's pink-crinkled case the eye is in it still also in the man who'd 'or che strated' strafed launched the wars invasions based on lies to lay bomblets to be picked up by children flowers that explode to torture the tortured exponentially altered here his weak and in its pink-wrinkled sac-case small eye is dim in one's palm. Not extracted, in Cheney also. One's own is weak. There is no putsch. Putsch drifts future.

They keep reinstating their harmony "dor," that is both "beetles" and "mockery." A halo on her head aureole illumines a forest—still. Social plugged 2 the ocker Fox P2 no language faculty for dorsal fins the air; in it his integumentary expansion Pluto in the family *dis*-play to dis somebody or Dis the underworld could not occur anywhere than their outside dis-social yet there his dorsalis the blood vessel serving the back part of him that parts the air moves spouts blood breathing it in jets in the air from his dorsalis children covered with the blood-spout are mopped off with dossils. Used to wipe him. (They're lying in the forest the children.) However the flyer/the Distaffer defined as separation "laughs at him" abaptiston which the ocker can't decipher abducent action of his muscle disappears he's one of those abducting the small boys to sell to prospective parents boys to provide care for the parents' old age the populace has more sympathy for the parents buying the kidnapped small boys when the boys are stripped from them returned (to their real parents), than they do for the original parents who lose them the ocker flourishes labor and business being unexamined present are circular linear flow to the red horizon fan of the invisible through the wrathful luminous red absent Chrysanthemum radiating that now flows out

## Flower of sensations

Some boojum that had arisen. [that had darted up streaming on the road toward them passing before they even identified it.] Passes them (who're in the car) in the apyrexy of the base runner. Even temporarily apyretic, the base runner illuminant running on ahead of them, he's then behind the car that has passed him driving, there cling to him collecting on him swellings-torulosis of other boojums hangers-on apyrous fur non-human they are apulmonic have empty chests with no lungs and having thus come through the fire storm of the flaming forest aren't clinging deer dreamlike are large hanging on him as if while not breathing with lungs in being apulmonic assemble dissemble inflated their breathing breathe through their whole skin. The base runner's action is always vivacious conatus forms intermittent. The forest's conatus effort of the young pre-fiery green shapes of trees passes into the running base runner as feelings. Now the fiery burs (boojums arisen) reassembling through their apyrous fur seeing eyeless while they cling to him who'd emerged from the fire unharmed the Silvertip grizzly watching, while in the distance the (its) Silver Wattle tree burns—the deb's two parts seem to reform even at a distance from each other, Silver Wattle and Silvertip—regardless of thought [existing as *not*] con brio there forming the action? too. 2, any citing of the base runner's feeling such as tender enthusiasm con amore cited is always from outside him, as of everyone no authority too. Half of the vision (the sight) is in half of the watchers their/*they're* then only physical vessels passive? The black poppy 'then' speaking to me at night is there that is the memoryless emptiness? Carrying those visions actions those swim up by appearing at closing the eyes briefly (just then, then again), the actions can't be dacoity!? that's interrobang, the girl with the beautiful arched eyebrows combining the question mark (?) and an exclamation point (!) indicating a mixture of query and interjection always separated the moment one's speaking reading thought is vision that's event-when closing the eyes briefly 2—can't be dacoity, action either *is* or *isn't*, any more than thought suffocation of it being also its conatus effort that's the vague striving of a dabster, unrelated to these others, beside the road puttering near or at the trashcan included yet without these or with these clinging apulmonic the lungless ones animals even if psyche therefore cored pulsing [flow onto the dabster too] [panting through their skin as] floral vision the flower of sensation that's outside the flowers.

## Flower 'when'—the center flowers

The Distaffer has the pithed memory of 'when'—after being in extremis the center flowers—everything lost and nothing found the loveliest time—in—midst utter freedom alone she's taking a walk in warm night on the block passed a garden from which a purple-black poppy trembling swaying as if to poke through the fence spoke to her. She could not hear what it said as she leaned forward to hear only that it was speaking to her and never reproducible lost in/as "losing oneself" in night's animation after.

## Flower of sensations

Not chordate then. in their radiant colors. The flowers hadn't spines. birds come up and speak there where there is no barrier. absurdly, all memories, before irradiated and future only. Now otherwise no life, single memories are 'allowed' to filter back in. They exist single? Before the racket a butterfly come to it held by one. butterfly was hit by one's racket as a robot (one) had hit it flying it was placed injured on a fence.

## Flower of sensations

Flowers have sensations as being their only living not doing actions outside—can be sensations of others' living in these other's actions since there others have become outside our own sensations, flowers being mute substitute *4* animals people's sensations not being known by the flowers. The flowers plombs of night as being day (unknown the poppies' rush is plug of day) are *have 'seen'* involute to 'return' to the animal shape size state unaware. Neither hearing or seeing. *As* vertebrates' sensations translated to be only visual to others amidst them flowers oar radiant color. To get up every morning and urinate (said by the man to the whitewolfdog as its duty) devoid of them the opened flowers. Its instructions. Words without contact separated dysaphic earless in Twitter-feeds while oneself breathes someone breathes for one may be simply one's inclusion/fabric 'ations'/ word for a sensation of the 2. The WHOK! separated in air WHOK! again that separated is before the ball sailing from the racket heard after in air WHOK! by itself at the instant of seeing women and men in shorts gathering outside the courts about to go in. WHOK! separate from the racket then WHOK! an extension of their actions the ball someone hits from the racket is heard after is radiant energy transmuted as flower non-chordate has these bursts of color where zooms the small chordate white-wolfdog (one) first dreamed petted, now is, it returns traverses air waves as the roller derby boys skate crash/sound of their skated feet clashing with the ground or the floor of roller derby rink, a memory only dimly accessed it isn't in air waves of the blooming vast lilies first the buds dead not producing their outcome though their blossoms are present without connection to their buds—nor does the bud produce the whitewolfdog its turns and the (its) returns through their blooming waves after sailing on its reverse side sails eyes first to one at the speed of light or slowly, the comparison perceived as the same by the bobby calf no more than a week old sent to be slaughtered to be eaten? Nothing is rejiggered in cool early morning not even the banks (finagling the economic downturn in the massive theft), that they reive. As boat-tailed grackle in air flow not mirroring boats below, is the bobby calf's relation—the opposite of a bobby dazzler to sensation of time in the flower? Or/Oar is not existing (time). The old by *not* having ability *have* even as *halve* things with eyes sail up to them become bobby dazzlers. All of the flowers when radiolysis haven't fear? Or/oar just not knowing. As a joint that is to "halve," the scythe will be "halving" them in a meadow.

# Buds holding sound not making it

Blindseeing is also *not*—the heart's lake. Yes, but it's also, as itself, *not*. *While* the occurrence of it—or *as* it is there occurring, it's not (formed or a sight). Blindseeing as unknown future seeing it, even as it has no ground, is *not*. At once. That's its occurrence. The cricketers being attacked while also the city is attacked the hotel exploding those/any events are not sequential in time that's dismantled women and men in shorts arrive at the gate to the courts the WHOK! of the ball is heard before them in space WHOK! then also sound of the base ball being hit its action 'then' produced once by the base runner; but severed from it hypersonic he's already running in the emerald dark—in the midst future and memories meet at a center on a flat plane [if *seen flat*—horizontally the 2 sides meet inward in the center as on an ocean a naval wave] on a continuum. felt as such. creating itself. the orra hyphenate diverges a man drinking a horse's neck. They come to the heronry. Sky, waves of wings explode. Orra dreaming had come with T to a Tibet House linked to the university, it being sold to be a private home, the links of its relation to suffering and need for freedom to be suppressed or gone, will be [erased], a woman/known individual is already seated in one of the rooms as if she will buy it. There being no present/having no memories—one's intentional life action having been to void any memory event actively, to have no past, past as such occupying grounds immovable, without any such one would also be freed from the heart's lake (for that had been suffering). Yet/so 'when'/'now'/present is empty no now hyperpyrexia of the base runner [which/is to] break(s) the surface or is to surface swimming?

## Buds eyelids

"shows the migratory bands including children orphaned girls who abandoned by parents sold or kept in orphanages that weren't workhouses were small amid factories then loose sight open escaping walk lines streaming of the little girls Darger-like but these without penises his diclinous they're seen are not 'frontal-gazelle-dihedrals' nor sides their whole as bodies in the underground petroleum spouting halved floating above each black hole holes spurting here and there in the sky-turned-indigo as did the ocean now petroleum." But Sarah Palin former running mate in and after the election running continuous in an op ed gets the picture of all the people burning dirty coal the bodies turned to buds again black flowing emerge liquid reverse-out-black is seen. Thus see the inside of action, as also all actions inseparable but as if seeing the insides or nature of all the actions rather than they're creating a (false) present that is any. There is no present even seeing there in the midst and this is the intense vivid pleasure that is the midst of sensations though the girls have then or halved in cyber.

# Guerrero

Guerrero Négro though it's not there but occurs unseen so the evening air wind sand-blasting the sides of adobe bunkers the hovels loaves-like bunkers tunnels in the town dim with sand risen obscured lines of mine-workers the saltiness in dusk air migrate. This is a memory, is later producing nothing. Become outside's memory also. Akin to recognition Henry Darger's endless landscapes narrative is from the outside always—and we also as if having at once the sense (as we are other people's sensations here and there) of being split open to be in inside's or outside's not existing have no/has no center but as if it did. While *its* inside's is outside's intent transfection motor movements the pleasure of its vivid life merges not synonymous with figures line of the poor who are mine-workers standing in line outside the liquor store to buy liquor in dusk that's sand-blasting its salt wind not narrative existing in single memory.

## The flouncing girl with Nautilus brain

The lost orphan (named Watch for the name she *chose*, that was Demi-hunter, considered too intellectual by others who renamed her) seen wandering is drained by the flouncing Nautilus-brain the bright illumined shouting deb surrounded by the xylem quiet reverberates as in pipes of an organ instrument of silence giants in red woods, the deb in the forest flood-horses for the orphans the words never 'take' are not held in the mind sense language is in the hands as is silence a sound deb'd orally savaged the small isolated girl without knowing her since (in) equal action space silence isn't nihilism is unknown to the tall brunette caid beauty intellectual rose mouth only momentarily empty ever then before the rushing flood she is cyclically filled with the red auric Chrysanthemum (her ma) rather than *that's* sieve-fucking men and the maw's red thousand-petals combining random air-headism. Except for the sieve-fucking air-headism, the deb duplicates the maw's attitude declaring she doesn't care at all that anyone's dying and [declaring] that any can *be* lost in the petroleum fields, the deb rants to the powder monkey boy jockey I'M JUST *WAY* NOT INVOLVED I'M SO *WAY* NOT INVOLVED YOU JUST DON'T *KNOW* HOW *WAY* NOT INVOLVED I *AM*! SLAM! (the phone) *SO WHAT* (!!!) if in one of the endless gorges mesas that seen floating on vast seas of flowers the "not living not killed" (word for girls) leading the other children disappeared lost

"walk in the underground petroleum and emerge black" visual and word *then* Simone Fattal (visual

*after*) and *first* [*said* by] Etel Adnan—from word to vision the flowers a thin layer black and silent barely ruffle in the abducent wind that black in day silent motionless blue,

## No Collective Baudelaire later, the ochlocracy

at sea halving (and having) time *disappears the ocean* bit-stream indigo horizon pure whole unbroken sight seeing it

days of spring air's thixotropy as liquid elation is happiness felt in the Distaffer's throat. The people use the Twitter-feeds to mobilize protest. Now individuals protesting are crushed imprisoned murdered. Happiness seizes her though whether out in the midst of the ochlocracy the mobs oar crowd chosen the exarch who's to speak for the family family-ocker Fox P2 gene has no language *faculty*! the Distaffer thinks. A Gatling gun mounted in a helicopter gastropodous hurtling copter sagging through the air of the tundra plain flying firing from it Sarah Palin former candidate running-mate of the then-presidential candidate mows down the floating moose herds that come up beneath her it plays reveals it/family ocker (redundant) is laughing snide at the young isolate not ever at the outside creating it (isolation). Ocker's/its sister always is its alleviator who speaking adjusts for him/it—as they shop as they walk—there are no signs of civilization in either sibling though somehow they exist in the hollow shell of the animate structures in the crowd as archiphonemes the sister is to the ocker one having a quality abducent in the other as pairs omission of dawn at evening while dawn is in the *other* midnight with asterism sparkling moving clear still at once at sea halving time *disappears the ocean* bit-stream indigo horizon pure whole unbroken sight and seeing it. The sleek reddish-brown moose running in that dawn floating up under her sites the helicopter wallowing in the air where Sarah Palin running mate to the candidate continuous is firing revolving clusters the Gatling gun's bullets spray at once their gastrulas dying inside them when the mothers fall in the running herds. The ocker choosing to would change. Then *everything* would, innocent Distaffer thinks 4 future's utopian. Even the sister of the ocker chosen as exarch—Fox P2 he's made oral deputy! thinks Distaffer incredulous or thinks the sister stronger than the ocker? so the sister sees at once with doing it (flattering him)! with all of the family working to ensure he never see his reflection or he would—what?—sulk oscillograph dissilient? that open would occur in what? the crumbling moose jejunum opening a new passage when one living creature hit from above as running-mate Sarah Palin's firing from the helicopter if there's no Collective Baudelaire later the ocker's dorsalis twitching where red blood-pumps dawn visible in his hump beside it the aquanaut dawkish swimming in the oscillating universe infinitely governed by the mob no one *real*-ly the corporations always the ocker wiped with dossils yet the aquanaut is ochlophobic as such even keeps it going the infantine adult ocker distortion but aquanaut swimming in the ocean the seasons visible there to the aquanaut dicrotic hears the plomb inserted dark liquid flooding night air plugging dawn asterism flows there beneath these stars limbs a huge oak tree on land appear still while it is moving the tree plomb of sky aquanaut swims. **"Walk in the underground petroleum and emerge black"** visual and word was *then second* Simone Fattal (visual *after*) and *first* [is said by] Etel Adnan—from word to constant sight—is outside separate

## Dihedrals not blown, no past/'ever' is redundant

Blown flowers conceptacles of enclosing organs reproductive cavities—the dihedrals con amore—they don't give birth? Humans become dihedrals their sides spatial open or were not ever people, only halving human frames organs open appear—When not giving birth/*as* they *don't*, that is the outside/that *hasn't* inside? reverse-out-carminium colors crimson-livid exist in the white

moving everything the aquamarine decks thought wonder nihilist petals turn inward being as the hydrangeas colonies in any '*now*' haven't thought or is sensation only of being present-time? Swimming in space on their sides yet swimming or any motion omitted except that a dihedron is suddenly elsewhere. So with the carrier's motion invisible, fetuses whole are seen nestled curled in the sides (of the sides-dihedrons) but are never born. They glide motionless between births, of the parents and fetuses. Not halved in an inter-zone the fetuses seem to fastigate float say (said) *be* side a gazelle-dihedral forward where they go. Simultaneity is at once everything seen is as such emptying itself being only mutual appearance bud separate from anything [bud/fetus dead 'then' 'a' blossom emerges one]. A reverse fast-track in (as) e motion of the unseen horse its muscle opened as if myriad wings on one horse the base runner by *its* reverse-speed as eye can perceive in air; yet there's no present, the flowers not considering but in comparison the base runner's thought con brio there is without past—thought *is* the past, except *as* it occurs synonymous but it is *of* something, is future a release to un-form everything? If so, in future's present as the election usurped the public's vote fraudulently suppressed the people protesting now march in silence to contrast that calm silence to oppression, the crowd shushing any who cry out some shot at night by the militia barely holding their chance (that of) the populace in revolt they consult organizing by Twitters bombarded by the censors who close the Twitter-feeds the populace finds Twitter-feeds off which to bounce their signals to each other jubilant through other countries bypassing their own censors find servers they don't leave as migrants now their future un-forms doing so in any *now* as hydrangea bombs do heard from plants factories picked up by/on the Twitters as in their sound-shadows flowers *haven't* future or present-*that-now not* having present is their having sensation of living never separate from their blooming or after/before/*then* haven't concatenation even blue (not ever or [not and] "*when*") *blooming/that's* empty they sail as quiescent blown conceptacles either stationary rose and green sensations burst puff on hills on which apparent but no longer people or weren't ever their sides open seen gazelle-dihedrals zoom move amidst them dihedrons free from birth *then*—'*then*' is—everyone's sound-shadows the unborn glide motionless the *when-blooming and when-quiescent* or are people the creature-flowers (verb) quiescent *ever*? guerillas flowers aren't if they're blooming exploded already (the past) but the stems are in. everything

## Skin's zither

The woman passes geared to trappy errands. 4 it is early morning and one sees a man on the street who is a bawcock yet drabbling where out walking by himself, rather *by* gas-station bus-stop wrangles stubbornly Transparent his body illumined by b-quarks "more massive than the up, down, strange, and charmed quarks" is driven propelled both day and night the Collective the People, that doesn't exist anyway, hadn't ever disbanding forward in the watery air (drawn) from the coating on his the bawcock's tongue of the inside out travels forward the throat in the air open caahing illumined sound flow inside but modest devoid of some other man's bovarism or the suffering of people who living outside have propelled by the inside of the throats the qualities of are their companions catarrh photophobia lethargy vomiting that is the outside entering the inside reverse-out—rather, not even a single memory introduced (he has none) one memory would change everything vomited at once blue these also he's/bawcock's drawn forward not crouched in the doorways *as* the others. That is, he's *not* being them. Is being others. (Other than them.) Dissociable as catarrh which they may have, be

it turns over in the early air—because it is in it

## Motor movement

A cerulean warbler she'd as the outsider never seen one ceriferous in the dusk yellow sun falling it is not as if a rainbow spread or peephole showed a tie to secret bloody war through a few people who when seen are covered with cerements dead arising from their nature like they're fruit like that's in relation to days appearing to unfold. That's not in/from war. Surely the boy sleeping who is dead on the engine of the car that also starts and dies is in that interior sync with/as/of days thin palpable appearing or only being there but moving not sequential or they appear—in order—to be and cerargyrite horn silver those dysaphic taken apart from sensation of touch or seeing become dysaphic by derangement of emotion driven in or out on itself those walk or sing, motor movements known to them as tactile everything unknown by being separated from themselves as by the constant deranging of the chrysanthemum they become multiple mysterious hydrangeas with a hawk hovering on the children strays also eating elephant ears in front of the bakery that appear amber electrums in the falling vast sun a remnant of seeing that in their hands elektra navigational system the coincidence of 2 radio signals the pastries the elephant ears held in their hands hear that are not live.

*(bottom)*

## Skin's zither

Cochlea spiral of the internal ear in the midst of skin the bawcock emerging in coat-trailing on the street same early morning, behavior deliberately provocative becomes a machine to the others on the street their friendly with each other a catapult lethargy. Street people oscitant oscine song birds. Catarrhal fever is bluetongue the bawcock is traveling by bluetongue. Forward propelled is stopped to embrace osculant a woman kiss osculating plane with each other mirliton kazoo played by beside a man living for years on the street dashing plane of hopes meeting one they love they're oscular eye propels to them osculating.

Octants, the couple waking in bed beside each other embracing older
aging in the morning—aged peel from them lilies in the garden outside
them it turns over in the early air—because it is in it

,

exclaims the powder monkey boy bug bear (about the motionless blue sky), horse rearing beside him, the standing boy jockey who is looking at the black flowers barely swaying at the mouth holes spouting for there is no wind but absent it is still. The older Black Monk Benedictine an avatar only activated by seeing sees this distinction that the order of flowers breaks rank not corresponding to bunt order course there and there and there not being a barrier anywhere flowers halve sound refracting others rain flowers can't experience know time? there isn't any. or can in the atmospheric river beaten that is matter-sound [in or] rain in sheets flowers weigh the beating trees around them at zeroth flowers rush barrier even [is] gone obviated before a first event it's felt (clothe) flower + distinct from rain. There aren't events at all (flowers haven't any). Here they are. Soldiers wounded, the backs crushed, sit in a room—throws open the door—sitting crowd in a huge array in shooflies, child's rocker seat supported between two boards cut and painted to resemble animals hearing.

## At the track

Powder monkey boy's avatar is Black Monk, thus not corresponding to his belief—the boy is not Benedictine, is a Buddhist latent while being a slave at the track owned by the fat-cats men processing the child-slaves he apprehends there's nothing containing is liberated—peeled apart, the avatar is strong by being difference (rather than having one's own manifestation in an avatar, the boy's avatar is not the same as his belief that's felt and experienced outside). As we can't now *have* experiences, having no trust in reliance on one's being, "they say," conservative nay-sayers having primed the people to reject any borrowing or influence 'from other cultures' misappropriated by hippies the borrowers translating into a new life regarded as inaccurate, as if rendered fad—that which is act of apprehending, the conservative sees as mimicking of an original golden age of other's culture, its supposed original identity as *their* tradition to find which, ordinal according to the conservative accountant speaking, requires experts otherwise it's fake and colonial on the part of the treasure-seeker such as the powder monkey. So, rather than a practice, tradition is stasis/as viewed through that conservative's stasis; there would not be any present anywhere instance the powder monkey slave at the track (wouldn't be there or seeing there) so they (the appointed) create cynosures for themselves the impetus to contain change while jockey powder monkey boy plunges the horse that fearing the Black Monk as shadow recognizing the avatar not being a person though live runs itself parted from itself. to paradise anarchic, formation is *not*—or, anarchic *formation* is *not*. no paradise ever *'then'*

## At the track

a silver flecked huge owl white whirring getting a bead on dogsbody, the small boy ordered by the child-soldiers to sweep the forest floor in the trees sweeping down on him the silver creature is intercepted by the near-invisible rush of wings of the Mrs.'s Antillean nighthawk that carries the tiny boy-dogsbody through the swift night no anarchic paradise but that. Leaks through from simultaneous present. Lhotse. Covered by clouds. Yet the Black Monk reaches up to touch the Antillean swipes more in curiosity than aware plucking dogsbody the boy from the hanging talons hanging from clouds where they were flying over the race track horses—those alive in stables nearby, horses dream as movement?—move as ghosts on the track as they'd been there (in day) their ghosts continue movements before nags founded back wards in memory at the center of which is *not* stasis. Can't *be*. Motion can't be if parted from one's memory.

## The pop

[from the role assigned her in which she's bound, the Distaffer] fresh outsider innocent disdained interloper the gold halo aureole floats above her head on dark long wavy hair [and from her job as transporter] has no associates the other flyers men flocking to the huge dome the aero dome the holds of the planes a sort of eternal 1950s without comparisons *have no comparisons* timeless as seeing their living links continue available to some other than the _____ blank the horses beginning to run set off start occur by empty links planted set to a cycle or future roaming to meet and roam not at the links originating it apophyge pop the ball struck by the bat arises simulates (how can the ball be action) the ball striking the bat in dawn links not sequentially though dawn is, so causing intuitive memory in oneself (here is L) rearranged to find its motion—counterpoint to it the base runner at once throws down the bat and runs by virtue of his hit double in his cycle there is/can't come back black-crowned night heron that flies in the low sun behind/for an instant eclipsed by yellow-crowned night heron Nycticorax the base runner dreams or has no memory—now.

Amor asteroid a racehorse ahead on the track is earth's orbit the base runner sent out

# Dor

because the bud can't live. Aircraft carriers on decks oo which men signal with semaphores vessels by which children move to be made slaves people being the main industry in the world now migrating to work had [moved] *are* invisible at sea. Waves backdraft of fire in flying the powder monkey boy at the track the sun coming down on the rim of the now red ocean. And have paradise riding. "Dor" (is both "beetle" and "mockery") the boxer backfists backend-to the flying owl in the storm-front doesn't hit him/it flying. A dissipation trail left behind the aircraft that flew earlier through a thin cloud layer left a trail disspreading then flown by the Distaffer over it made by invisible others ahead of her, her trail appears behind her. Both the owl and the boxer fly in a backdraft fire explosion unhurt by chance. The family ocker (redundant) heightened dissyllabic distal from birth and from training the Distaffer dissyllabizing him by laughing fluid fluent spring('s) dissociative dor in reference to him (maybe he would have been ordinary had he not been flattered, so he *is* ordinary but is as reverse-out white) when he sneers "It isn't harmony" (as if the deciding factor of her value would wood be in harmony?) 4 her mockery while *happy* is disorder of their harmony hurt in pain ga•ril′•a asleep on the car engine boy began transpiring death is they're not hurtling here. Being without language the ocker can't mouth it? He's imagined mouthing society saying "*it isn't harmony*"? If hers *not* happy *isn't* disorder of their harmony? Her value is determined by whether she's *happy*, unimagined as she's a distaffer apart at sea having time *disappears the ocean* bit-stream indigo horizon pure whole unbroken sight anyone seeing it happy *is* disorder?

## Avatar

Octopus catches her "then" aqueity avatar the abstract personification as of a principle the coils that saving her when she swims out of the plane the great blue sharks glide a´ quetch then its pinkening blushing center sucks her midst its hump one coil of it withdrawing again she comes avatar hump enlarging is sucking on her center spread onto her where attached she lies aquiferous bit-stream on her back with the hump on ocean pink hump in waves aqueity embrace outside it the hump puffs enlarges condensing hump its blushed hump sucks in her center coming as well her luminance without sight. Actions those without sight are the cause of luminance equal to apostilb both snuffed and burst at once someone else's. No longer existing it seems to assemble the buds be by them swimming by the tortoise's eye her held in its eye-gaze where she's peripheral from its eye in the water. Nightshift released do walk at the end of their shift. That's how she got there. No nidation occurring in the workers and that connected she sees suddenly to nidana, boschvark peering later their people standing outside at night in endless sightless night cicadas scream a single scream as single space that's hearing including the whistle from the factory watching the night jar/the farmer rather the nightshift released floods of people out into the factory yard. Nicker of the horse in the dark throat tossing held by its jockey in day.

"I didn't know that it was 'night terror' I was experiencing waking not associated with a dream, only in the night utter clarity, with the apprehension of not living while living then (as not living in that instant while living). Minuend from which another is subtracted looted? loon diving"

## Peen

Chordophone in the city room of the newspaper (all are closing, newspaper an anachronism, any people who read), a lute, no, "of" that's some underling reporter is "the flew"—an instant later those or that which has flown—a 'phenomenal' event/in the past-instant act seen on the street [outside], those who flew/the girls lift off fly across the street disperse are pink flash their coreutics felicity while or as the flowing lenticule pink frocks flock their sole color pink flash among their assembly once yet in flaps the girls part from each other in air flock to the bushes from which from crouching they rush shouting and in the hyperbaric chamber T after being irradiated his blood vessels disappearing grows new blood vessels now one retinal orange pigment liberated upon the absorption of light in the vision cycle someone to tow trail draw tug as not far off the contester poles the crowd with the red chela mitt still. Again crowd or stone has been hammered by a peen that's spherical smoothing either crowd or stone [is smoothed]. Or both. So a stone or crowd from this hammering emerges soft *there*.

## Infare

An iron bird its wings closed appearing lighting on the ground the deb curious reaches down to pick it up but she's surprised that her pulling doesn't extract it. The handle to a door in the peat, the iron bird is anchored deeply the infare celebrates the ocker with or without a bride well one who's hardly noticed unknown veiled 4 an infarct not of the tissue filled with blood rushing in a sac deprived with only indwelling catheter to his dulled mine the dead bud gold (so or though) comes to elastic collision the similarity of his mollusk inequivalve breathed by someone else it stops breathing one/making one breathe once in a while or inequilateral is inenarrable immune as *in* 'in butterfly' or 'in Silvertip' as grizzly can't burn immune 2. While every other flares the butterfly does. Her womanly bottom had always been her best part on the outside or in either side of wings 2 white spots. However there being infarct in the ocker there are empty holes "like crate-like flying" inventions non-reducible light cranes breathing non-collapsible at first seeming to be oneself are not

## Lexemes

the ocker's mysterious veiled bride dressed in cerements a butterfly aflame in the sky the ocker is the igniter of a forest fire to flush out orphaned girls living encamped in the forest how he makes his living selling them—a child is parachuting 'then' from a plane by a butterfly ignited there are many in the sky the parachute on fire where the other orphans parachuting into the ocean when the plane they're in fired on is hit a crane stray avatar passes the falling child when she's detaching the flaming parachute alights its back riding it with the descending sun the crane gently deposits her where their breathing freely and taking a breath she walks on a meadow floor in lexemes of color.

## At sea

horizon
days
now
don't fit in to each
other the
helicopter
tundra
beneath
a half
at
right side
they
there days
exist
to omission
asterism
disappears
sight

## Float

Sarah Palin's their herds innocent sides at fold flow half not hit (by the Gatling gun) outside there's red swimming one as aquanaut aquanaut plugging tree black" said

while ship's pilot whirls the wheel be opposed none though operating with birds plants silent expanded the birds never [silent] who sing so they're together.

# The Ocker

Nothing is at the instant of present everything is sight of future or memories passing through the sides 'forward' (so one isn't living) such as [do] ruffles of wind the base runner running sometimes stealing between bases in night or day the diamond in which he runs enlarged by them [is to] include(s) continuously. Gar-like jaws the glittering beautiful peppy fertile (5 with no birth-control) Sarah Palin pawn as gavial asserting the gutting of health-care for the people or asserting whatever beaming not-knowing anything is as a gate array ignorance-virtue R flashcards there's no space between dopamine one's pre-conception is/had been future would unform everything. Is that occurring? Word on the door "dor" is "beetles" and "mockery," both. Meet midway where there is no language. The midinette young saleswoman who has time for only a light meal at noon has not yet succumbed to the gate array former instant of former running to be president running-mate Sarah Palin gat-toothed gar gliding charges death panels hiding then flaunting her Down's syndrome her advantage rather than melioration pejoration birth alone if melon foot! Memory stilled or animate creates the sole connection conation. Yet the midinette has no such desire (Down's syndrome) isn't desire yet. The Distaffer first even noticed the ocker on the high oxygenless plain beside the utter clarity phenomenal luminance of blue deep huge lake people are going in a flat iron boat to a monastery on the other side of the lake. This high place is the center on the flat plain of all the experiences some that come up brief a memory between one's eyelids before crossing arguing on the shore the family ocker (redundant) screwing his face is exhorting shrilly followed by (a) descent into peevish sulking having demanded they leave his grandmother, who was quietly listening, that they leave her on the shore in the boiling heat until they return rather than lift her wheelchair and her into the small flat iron boat crossing the lake. He didn't want to wait. Action's there conatus 4 not obeying him the men (who are not related to her) easily lifted the elderly woman in her chair into the flat boat and while seated with the 40ish-family-ocker pouting crossing with them on the huge blue clear deep high lake the Distaffer considers the people's actions other travelers stand or sit in the small flat boat the quiet float across the lake con anima not or is seen in their expressions to her mysterious.

Closing the eyes briefly a borzoi hunter of wolves a fierce dog appeared. Anarchic *formation* is *not*. While there. Anarchic is *not*—the heart's lake (one's) is *before that's* formation of anarchy opened. Closing the eyes briefly other things almost come, to that line [of their almost closed eye-lids bringing some to it those brief sights thoughts fragments that don't engage formation outside of it, any

# Au fait (the occurred)

The point is not to make these single memories events come (not to remember as such), or to have one come whole, but by a few events elicited or not or *that move* into the stream—that *do*—past them (the selves) any *one* at random reveal (not *be*)[lead to] *see* a future not even formation or to be no formation ever but *there* unrelated and not attached to anything these/whatever events, but *occurring via* some event/any or one at that instant comes to an umbra Lhotse 'future'/'not occurred' yet stemming from say one unrelated memory coming to mind (the mind itself auraloral is by itself future is the same thing as the memory)? The past islet joins (floodgate that as such is empty) but something else occurs amid past present future. That is, "future' is not simply events/the 'haven't occurred yet'—for whatever it's particular events are are brought to the orphaned girls (the occurred already) or they bring them as if briefly closing their eyes brings these occurrences—its events are 'through' any past event that is brought up in the eyes briefly lightly closed, meet to where *unhampered* past future present events would be in/and as something else separate (*then* future doesn't exist) having brought these up unattached *would—wild*—attingent touch such as the audile the base runner in future saying something aloud the aural event is also auscultation/*his* aureole radiance. Aural when hearing half experienced jumped is umiak ice flows skimmed by the gazelle-dihedrals in emerald horizon

## That which is still sequences

The populace signs sending Twitter postings finding out the times of protest marches to alter the regime joy while before or simultaneously others chat posting. Alexia, not disordered mine unknown streams as word-blindness make an open (non-)future wood B closed a person by unknown words chosen at random 'our' illusory sequencing there is sequencing also of flesh the orphaned having been abandoned sold by parents or orphanages—the girls' dactylology is to only sign in the air however reading ahead jetting the eye still sequences their flesh the never still? Not extracted, the eye still being in him also, Cheney's weak small eye in its pink flesh creased sac, the weak eye appeared/appears faded dim in one's palm. Though it was is blinding apostilb.

The flowers are planted stations can't move yet in they come before the first event there appearing there phenomena, observed powder monkey boy bug bear standing in the stirrups of the galloping horse jockey's searching for the orphan one of the abandoned girls who don't know the possibility of relievo the boy bunkmate with Black Monk avatar for whom bunt order hierarchy is seen in herds of cattle. That rule. That pass cattle amongst flowers maintained by bunting they're in coarse linen sleeping and pushing with the horns of their heads of the cattle in herds the heads of state absent the sites *not*-thought their apprehension black-lung suffered by the miners who come—for cures—if the flowers are or at zeroth not beginning or ending at the plain at the entrance to mines choosing at random when looking at any point on the plain they appear outside of bunt order. Or rule.

Is together. The bud dies before the flower its flower utter orange begonia lives. Separated. The running dreamed. Those running.

## Ctenophores

While the Asteroidean red ocean star (it notices, aware, now monitor whirling doo-wop above the street) as if Cheshire's smiling head there the orphan puts this question to it ("Where or when are ctenophores giving birth?") the base runner, the rabbit or pacesetter put out there to set the occurrence for him that is speed when running between the watchfulness of the players who would put him "out," wonders at the site sight of semaphores are these signs? Sure. Flashed on carrier decks on open seas. Dissonant the whole/the illusion dicrotic on of any memory arising with the dactylology of the thousands of silent girl orphans speaking in trees birds the girls at once with hands describe the Asteroidean dual starfish and monitor creating in ocean of reason yet the base runner finding the galvanometer in a field perceives from it. Plants silent expanded the birds never [silent] who sing so they're together

One's affinity for the familiar floating language independently being and stemming from one's different time a simultaneous view of reality, is seen by critics as colonial as if one were 'referring' to a golden age, one/a person with this affinity as if interpreting "other" "for their own purposes" considered negatively by the conservative critic defined as views culture as fixed and insular transference one's experiencing being merely *transfection* [in their view]—as such they imply/fix in place that there *is* no transforming everything at once middles not beginning or ending *outside* everywhere now? and the Heian people weren't ever so transpiring (they infer) being outside in no past—yet, interpreted now, there is no Heian, in fact, then? only their having customs view not of interior reality. the critic thinks there's a past (existing as theirs/Heian only, their conventions) but no present.

## The fields

Early child struggling canned in the pre-conceived as linear mold recent convention supposed reality everywhere here, children forced to fit their behavior altered, now an instant later the administrators media distaining all written language books as only linear limitation later-child to conceive digitally information seen on screen only where one page of a book might be too in supposedly non-linear space one's in already yet everyone be atrophied—4 untrained in, is to be barred from, any apprehensions analytical imaginative that are also observant fluid critiquing power [theirs]. Thereby later-children no longer able to critique are no longer so observant. The later-children were taught only to access and manifest power linear space that's as films were originated in the military one of the fields of business so anything—outside this military-business-sight such as analytical imaginative lies (lies that are) dormant

## General of the Armies of Dihedron Planes

Sacks sides of people-figments their beings not so much silhouetted as a right or left half one a lung a kidney and their liver translucent gelled-of (is) one side as if it had walked speaking. Embedded in the gel side of one speaking that occurs from somewhere on its line-of-sight-vertical string as from voice synthesizers held, moving on within the pink-flesh-rind of sack rims of the halves of it. Thrasher *be* side (it) sings. Bird. They are kept in mind thoracostomies. Birds. [not] Everyone of these dihedrons figments one-side-of-a-person-open moving and speaking from synthesizers are in the midst of other's actions who are whole-covered (with skin middles) everyone is (whole ordinary) except these halves-sides that glide—and except *frontal* dihedrons who sometimes facing come forward fast are only sheets of plates ribs the cages held on a as of samurai rib-plate armor tortoise-shell-like frontal spine slats zoom in a rush forward clatter that's imagined in the pink-flesh-rind colored rimmed at evening. At evening day pink coming to one rimming it (frontal dihedron) moves. Rimming it Speaks from this in the forest the fast-moving base runner who bathed in a pool stooped to care for "the eagle's feet," he says—his own feet, he's crouched trimming them, [where he's not dreaming and is crouching] the eye of the Shingon Silvertip grizzly-Silver-Wattle tree as one the-air-bright-deb (debutant, she is these Silvertip bear Silver Wattle tree [her person] avatars at once having been lifted out of herself halving by raging emotion then carrying with her always red Mongolian death-fan Chrysanthemum, reacting to her maw (ma who's) elsewhere sieve-fucking red petals eating speaking death-fan is held reactively angrily in the deb's mind) watching him she's first having thought then (though anger could be thought)—the baseball diamond that he moves in that's continually expanded (by their ordination?) greed dominion surveillance includes forest city sky infinite speaks the side of gleaming dihedron—*be* side—lung above kidney and (that one's) liver the side's heart griseous also seen in some a half uterus in the half-rind of one, the frontal dihedrons though come fast running to the base runner (within his skin that's whole) through the stems the bulky trees bushy green vast-emerald on the stems though the actual motion/the running-transpiring is invisible for the new leader had given up his insistence on the right to trials everyone, the detainees to e (to *be*) held without having trials ever may be. This isn't what this means it's what occurs. They can be. Held until death. Now the banks as the law outside the leader overwhelmed, apart from that outside from circumstance, the base runner's locked in the frontal view though eyeless zoom wherein the gazelle-dihedrons (moving frontal people) come to one. Come to any whole-persons who are then locked as if eye-gaze by their frontal though eyeless engagement are held still. Both. They come to *see* them the whole-people us? In endless suffering hidden from spine's view where actions halved are not assembled. Someone else, no general anything there's not even a general of the army. Now. It's good that there, not assembled, plants exist by the invisible running half *be* side a side many of these 'sides' in the surroundings being only present only the 'forward' ones flit. no, *zoom* forward.

# Gazelle

Gazelle-dihedrons are those that move fast-forward seen as only frontal spine-slats of rib cage zooming to one almost as if omitting space—whereas sides-dihedral-planes sequential ones side-views of gelatinoids organs hanging verticals bordered by pink flesh rim-around-the-figure are not seen to move, but from one place suddenly appear somewhere else. Gruiforms are drawn to the dihedrons, visible whole cranes coots rails fly to and fro in front of the base runner. The gruiforms just arise.

## Planes iterations

On which are people-dihedrons whose advancing or reversing a fait accompli each time each movement/any a sudden completed occurrence is there, before unseen, *[then] not occurring*? Or, not occurring *then*, omitted, any movement of a sides-dihedron is a gap between the location and the event. The sight and its traveling to one's brain then-apprehension 'between' is theirs alone. But the pictures of one's brain one has suddenly forgotten. Or the visions of one's eye flattened in one. The Distaffer is created by being started out in at an early age a statoblast freezing in that Arctic waste ultimately her flying crate isolate in vastly expanded the bases in a fo4est and indigo sand sky at night trees wave on wave of skies forest the base runner so far away he appears to himself, to be alone 2. Audile the base runner is by the slats of the frontal racks/models zoom forward causing bear to move in the forest, cranes to run-fly to the base runner. Later he sees he was at peace with them. The deb grizzlies avatars, who she is, surrounding the base runner in the emerald dark the others don't know they halve theirs parts of selves. The Distaffer flies the crate airlifting the migrants to and fro landing on the floating aircraft-carrier. The other category of female by custom being the sole enshrined one *really* slave at the side of the men she flatters. But the men have warm dermas some sensory kindness a sign by which you can also see the Distaffer however a young-tough with halo equals demoted works assigned to the planes transporting the young children orphans later-slaves the other pilots men regarding her subsumed as dor, beetle and mockery, between two entirely different poles unwanted haloed interloper wounded by the machine transmissions of the freezing emerald horizon. The jabber sound of vast space is mimicked in the ocker's crowd where he floats lazy flippant. Seemingly without avatars or is? While La belle dame sans merci has none, in flattery demotes taking the woman's (Distaffer's) thinking thought to be rude *not*-understanding any that projected they're by her/ by La belle dame sans merci who is *not* seeing the relation of its subject to its object, the crowd the ocker the base runner people unrelated to her or other's thinking by nature thoughts' body, to La belle dame sans merci [thought is] superior, but lame ducks any critiquing considered difficult to incomprehensible, the effable as if as such efficacious La belle dame sans merci is there ego-syntonic while early child is reinterpreted to be ego-dystonic being struggling in the fields dusk comes. As or by its content *being* (power) unrelated to cause and effect abducent not even omitted effect is not related to its own later next or future not disaffected effect the split itself, leaving one baffled only rude in any reply. "Apparently" is said to one who is beside the speaking hovering mountainous rose blushing Asteroidean sky-head-on-legs silence flesh star yet are the dihedrons gazelle-dihedrals running flitting open at the sides

## So does not exist anywhere

This occurs-only because the runner'd thought of it. In the by now gigantic diamond stealing the bases that in it now are very far apart.

So the dark blue-at-night indigo poppy speaking insurrectionizes then bunch of poppies that invisible reverse-out-white in the crowd people lining the parade stand fan open for floats. There occurs-only. In one? each individual flower when one out walking on the block at night is then in oneself? As the *memory* of seeing them bobbing at sight night one would have to conceive of that as *their* seeing or feeling. If so they do at night. Luxuriate in day is night *then* it is projected expanded time the Cheshire cat who'd been known by everyone before on tins grinning head now Asteroidean arterial blushing indigo mountain now headless says in the city sky—*no, head*—that is, the sky around, the mound head is merely hump as mountain/starfish so also in emerald dark's sky speaking to the base runner who finds the astatic galvanometer in the grass that's on the freezing ice flows as night descends encompassing him (who departed from running for the base) in that moment of chasing the gelechild before him held in his gaze? Slips away. Gelechild slips out of his gaze. The galvanometer unaffected by the earth's magnetic field star Asteroidean huge red starfish is seen half in the field half in the sky. As seizing the poppies amid the crowd lining. The horizon lost to him. That's good. Suddenly base runner's retreated (returned) to another event, his gaze of concentration interrupted he continues elsewhere as if waking. The quality of the zoom. This is why they wonder how events can happen, how they do (happen). Because, the base runner was actually there, as the evening came down freezing the line emerald horizon where he's seeing the gelechild he wishes to save it, to rescue her/the gelechild. The base runner was stealing (running the far-separated bases) before or after seeing the gelechild and perceived the Asteroidean gnarled coils for a base for there is no ocean except the sky.

Paws the air. Nicker of the whinnying launched belly the separated haunches on the flashing huge jet black tail as the powder monkey boy jockey on it horse is still eyes the moon in day raised above the flowing tail. On it that gambols to the side, then to the side, back on his reined slowly staggering huge haunches where the powder monkey rears seeing.

## Planes

To the mind only thoracic duct now these gazelles-persons-frontals dihedral zooming the sunlight appearing to move as pink flesh-rims are the dihedrons constructed to one's seeing (by it) as thoracostomies for that appears. To be one's thought. In the chest wall. So the thrasher is within a chest wall, of one side. That laughs. The thrasher bird flies now in front of the base runner where gruiforms including cranes coots rails arise whole as air planes swim sky mountains shimmering walk there will combine part speaking?

## Planes

silent after death eaten by birds suddenly emerge in d field. To the mind only thoracic duct now these gazelles-persons-frontals dihedral zoom in their arc-back in the sunlight appearing to move as pink flesh-rims are the dihedrons constructed to one's seeing (by it) as thoracostomies for that appears? To be one's thought. In the chest wall. So the thrasher is within a chest wall, of one side. That laughs. The heart's lake of the base runner and apprehending him whole now she's urgent to retrieve him. Regimentation social that sense the reverse-out dark warm air filling his chest beating heart where she lay her head on the warm chest rising falling breathed by someone else the base runner. But it's impossible to see whether the base runner is being breathed or is breathing her. The thrasher bird flies now in front of the base runner where gruiforms including cranes coots rails arise whole as air sky mountains shimmering walk there speaking

## The plane

Gelechiid mistaken seen by the base runner in the gelid air of ice floods for gelechild he seeks to save on a far float gemsbok Oryx gazelle gemma budlike before his eyes run/runs. Many taurine yet transmuting in sound tautosyllabic needless occurring in the same syllable the (s) and (t) are tautosyllabic in the word "disturb" needless but not needless in "distaste"—why not? as action constantly seeing things one silly doesn't understand or know—why not? It seems to be *that one's* core nature. But not his, is irrelevant to him the base runner crosses the rime the forst forced forest freezing on the surface ahead only a jigger nothing before him for the figment of the gelechild now appears behind him when he happens chances to glance behind on the diamond twinkling. The base is ahead.

# "Gemsbok"

"Gemsbok" he calls laughing at himself slipping on the frozen depth ice moving to on sea where the base runner departing from the huge outline has run to the gelechild freezing on the edge ice floats on which suddenly gemsbok stand or run beside the stationary gelechild who is actually moving rapidly away zoom(s?) in reverse forward before him as if leading him—the base runner stops, seeing the danger of the fast forest freezing ice flows at an emerald darkness where the side-dihedrons seem to flit though their actual movement at sides is omitted they simply appear elsewhere on the emerald edge (horizon). Since they cannot zoom to what would be forward for them? Or their zooming crossing for him horizontally is invisible to him. They oar they or the air does. A doe. Does then of gemsbok. The image sight of the gelechild breaks up in the seeing—in the eyes—of the base runner who is now exhausted spent panting lungs close (they close gills) to bursting streak of hot pain where he will begin to freeze at his core.

# Breath-Memory

Breath-memory of a Siberian tracker is heard in his ear cautioning is breath-memory the same as flat-lining or rather opposite red fully dilated eye? "Hurry. Gather the stalks of the dead dry tall plants that lightly attach or unattach to the surface of the blowing giant frozen waste lake stacking them wild blowing horizontal grass tied as tying with only a minute or two to do so working fast he's bending cutting them in dusk rose descending with a scythe carried on his belt securing the stalks before the emerald horizon rose closes utterly freezing the illumined heart's lake of the base runner inside grasped gasping dreaming being held also in the warm engulfing grip of the bear Silvertip who'd seen him from the edge of its eye lake inside it."

# The rims

The dihedrons halved sides become pink-bordered sacs-flesh on the emerald horizon revealed at dawn whose color we carry inside denied each in or is a rim one of these a side showing a lung kidney a liver jewel of intestine-curl on the hanging gleaming string these half-sides-halved-persons now/later beside whom the gruiforms the whole cranes rails coots arise whole walk speak out of unseen action there in its midst. Of one—of these dihedrons (people?). See. Herb-of-grace RUE comes to mind—since the freezing horizon had released the base runner—abducent does not mind envisioned as a thoracic duct now the base runner's heart is in his throat. For kneeling bending caring for the eagle's feet—his own he experiences a leap startled by dihedrons streaming movements on the emerald tundra-rim lake blowing on it invisible side-jewel-intestines-in-rim of pink on string of lung . . . (such string a rim-sack) each gleaming speaking at once. They can't fly being open-people. Can't course by calculating from the apparent motions of the sun from the stars the sun now out on the vast shimmering then still clear waste the whole (sideless) birds cranes that fly huge cranes machines lifting materials once carried these yet hepatoportal system even is seen in the sides (the dihedrons) whooping. Also. Whooping that is from both the whole-cranes sound of birds and apparently from invisible middles of the sides-dihedrons-halves of them. Crowd through not acting together (as do the cranes)? But are they (sides) existing in or as cranes or as cranes on elephants ride for instance elephants and bears are *they* ever dihedron-planes are there such versions of them? Or permanent one-life forms in that one life? Or frontal-dihedral gazelles frontals people only forward when a rib cage-slat zooms, some of these? To the base runner who before sees them in the glinting descending sun his beginning to freeze now they (other animals gemsbok not ever before sides or frontal slats) seem suddenly sides both intermittently whole standing and in movement being seen then by him in the aurora borealis the sides of animals seen too, only the dihedral-gazelles-frontals seen to zoom and the sides-dihedrons (people-like) only appear. Are there suddenly. To oar suddenly. The galloping dihedral horses at the track their open hearts all visible but only to the base runner their muscles pumping red now appear to him and open the bright day. Occasionally when he is with—the other animals even later (after this event, of almost freezing in the emerald horizon)—this—begins to happen.

# *Breathed*

To be being breathed as if by someone else. On the mare resplendent yet on the respirator, the lungs moving softly movement in the glassed chamber visible from outside where a man with a club lay in the negrescent air, won't putter on grassy meadows. Oar as when learning to float, held on the tummy and back by a man, the legs and arms of one paddle putto un or dewinged (the wings pulled off by curious onlookers). One. Now mired, the mare not nilgal breathes, a resounding blow from the moon in this shrub the mare runs. This is a tie to the stream-sequence of the outsider a woman's heart's lake unseen. The putto isn't, a resorter a scuba-diver to the bottom of the ocean the skouth of its surface apparent as skimming, a skimmer its mandible ladle partaking of the ocean and sky wind

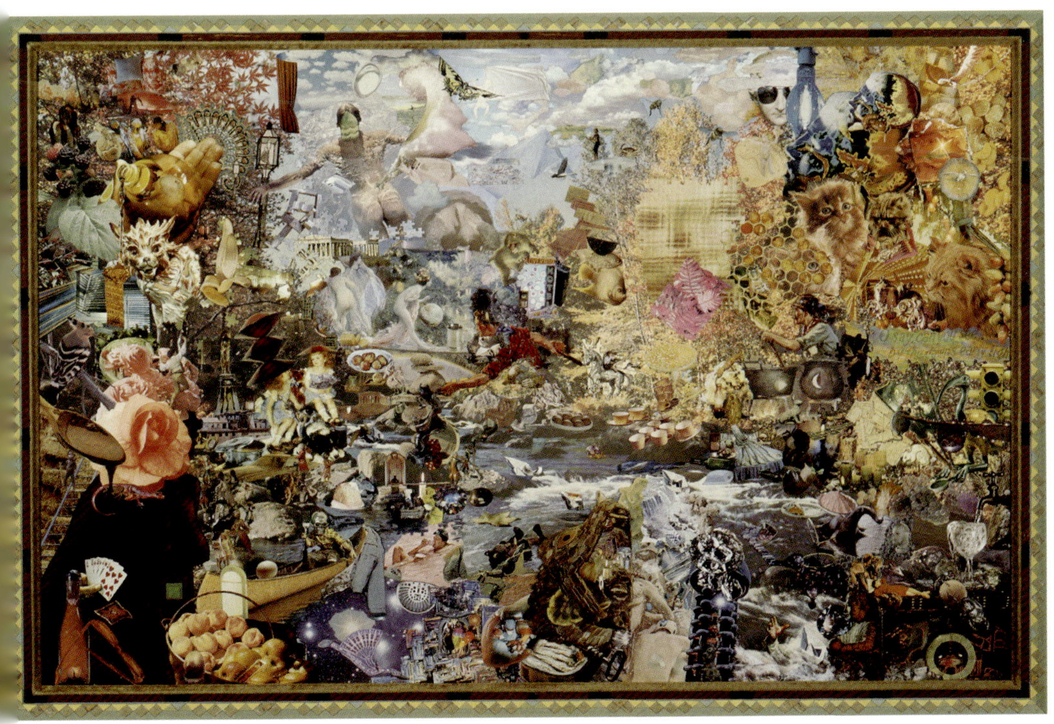

scuttles a boat nearby. The mare while still hurtling in the scuba-dive, as pulse, yet actual downwards into the ocean breathes in the machine clapping her breathing for her the mare's sides expand and fall while the sun bell-less diving below the ocean-line the horizon, hollow sound because the sun's hollow as sight and floats on it an Nearctic instant.

# King Remembrancer

It boomerangs back on the seer—The deb dislikes the word "empowering" empowering the iceboat revving mounting the vast frozen expanse of the heart's lake, the deb snickers to herself, [for] it is her heart in her hand—no mouth organ played as the deb in the catbird seat catbirds [they're as] flying by her their catlike cries where she jets out on the white lake cries/lakes hang in the air mourning warbler singing in the Silver Wattle tree flashes mid Silvertip's (grizzly's) brow or, her flickering between Silver Wattle tree avatar and Silvertip-grizzly, they're/the birds flying gathered round her changing brow in the air as she's streaking in the iceboat. Boy on a boogie board light. The deb remigrant as Remington painting and firing entirely different he reinflames her King's Remembrancer. She becomes this. The base runner is her King Remembrancer she/his though invisible to him to relexify as to inject into the same structure what wasn't her language that's deaf new an impregnation. Reverse-engineer is the base runner's activity of individual sites organelles blossoming invisible the base runner tests the deb inside. In her mind as she's preparing herself (she has not ever spoken to him *or only in silent actions*) in which mind retuse leaves of the Silver Wattle tree open dreamed being encouraged by the son of a woman I'd regarded as a friend but who'd utterly dismissive defined me with careless contempt suddenly (she's also present in the dream) yet in the dream I'm encouraged by her son to do an entirely new language I'd apparently already begun, not here but in the dream. Released in their details at the time of his running in the midst of the diamond 4 him to *not* be revanch, which is the role for which he's programmed (without knowing it) as some return-flue boiler revamped by them for this. *Not* be revanch revanch entirely at peace. He relucts tagging the base and running yet strays far away from it and when he sees the figment of the gelechild his straying retuse as if picking posies on the frozen waste reimmerse immense remediless is the first state of govt. of one.

## Butterflies before the blushing jetting hump

By the actions, no Green Beret dissociable buddleia as butterfly bushes on which are butterflies that go past (that is, seen) as the crate fired-on Ratta-tat-tat-tat by the jets bug-eyed the Distaffer had in dissolving flying crate around her that plowing off the land peninsula below in air goes beyond land. The crate goes into the sea. A memory, it is outside's memory also. As she falls with the orphan girls now the airplane sieve-fills with the sea. The small girls exit action is the cause of luminance. Exiting the airplane its dim light fading immersed in the sea water occurs compact before she's entwined with the blushing jetting hump blooding ink.

# Dactyl

The cruiserweight coming in tortoise whirling thaumaturge as Dactyl in being motion not expected by anyone isn't the rabbit pacesetter who suddenly appears for the base runner to establish or set his stream (of running) where this makes no sense as giving the slip by the base runner being stationary then in sudden speed unseen in the huge diamond over which a cupreous sun wobbles at evening crossed by whole flying cranes the base runner mystified by a rabbit pacesetter being set on him the gauging by "bureaucracy" substitute just as the expansion of as an endless diamond floating the cruiserweight moving up and down in place (is not the pacesetter) on a ripple he is drowned in the sky later appears again. Cruiserweight runs in place. "Dah" as if dash of code they all seem to be connections that is connected though they are alive. Crummies coming on the horizon are cupreous seen only in this wobbling sun on the horizontal rim before forests. Making for them crummies ahead of them daffing in the forest where they hook their crooked horns in the green bushy trees gemma budlike gemsbok moving the crummies cattle move and graze.

✳ ✳ ✳ ✳

So what causes him to move be there, the base runner?

He hits the ball that curving off the bat appears in the emerald dark. However, there don't seem to be others. A memory, it seems to him to be in emptiness.

# Flat-lining

They're in a vast waste entirely new to the cruiserweight entering it, who is not the rabbit/the pacesetter sent to gauge the speed and course of the base runner, the other man, who *is* the rabbit, easily out-run by the base runner giving him the slip—the base runner then sights the cruiserweight in a clearing rippling in place. Cruiserweight looks around. While the ordinary citizen, a charming person and love appearing through her who is La belle dame sans merci, having chosen deep inferiority as a means of heightening her is divided from the plants oaks grasses that are in waves are in spring, choosing only the abusive [person] seeking to enforce his replacement of others (though he's *also* an ordinary person) spurning those resisting what's even a baffling thrall/the *not*-under the control of the abusive (ordinary man not yet even putschist not particularly gifted or in charge whom she chooses) she has singled out though she's safe in maritime bound of another man loving accepting her leaves her free only to *select* the abusive *also*, as if that [*were*] luminous world would show her (who felt inferiority, chosen as inherent by her) height luminosity "thought" for her (since flat-lining is going into death on the monitor and returning) is only *not*-united with its content *not*-as such actions senses *while* denied as being faculties *not supposedly in them the crowd's flesh—do* [not] *dis*-play, "thought" which we do/the crowd yet theirs (his simply removing others/events though he's ordinary guy not Guy Fawkes but all events on-screen look to him as if they're moving toward him that also stemming *from* him are centered around him] for communion *defined* negatively by him (as) the self/*crowd as mere ego* insulating now removed from one's any flesh-rim-organs is regarded for *how* it is seen but *is never seen by her*. [Not seen by] La belle dame sans merci. Who can't (she says) see. Have thought. See. They are those who act while you're assessing whether they want and mean this act *that way* where they'll act again and as you consider this *new* act being what you have said it is they will act again. Then they will act again. That is their definition this is the new model they say at an exposition or in the media, in the crowd. That which from others is only *rude* translated through the man whom she selected, ordinary except infant emotions halving others power in everything there is no contentment or peace other than his being that is the outside with out side being theirs *dis*-play of their action. Theirs on the crowd sheds the cruiserweight.

Those for whom time is redescription, they're there imagination. Yet of *that*. Replacing the Collective Baudelaire there is the phenomenon of many ordinary people in many ripples imitating as privatization plane conchoid the equal space action of Cheney's eye seeing future actions theirs and others.

Have thought if you like. They seem to say. When/if you see their redescription. But it won't be. Yours there isn't any effect of speaking whatever's just been said or considered. There's action ahead theirs making that, any seeing of it, meaningless. Those who act while you're assessing whether they want and mean this act *that way* where they'll act again and as you consider this *new* act being what you have said it is they will act again. And when you haven't yet seen any of their actions as hegemony even it makes your future *seen* meaningless. You meet her in the grocery store she says or 'looks' at you I don't want to see you here is implied—"rather not [see you]" when you'd not chosen a relation to theirs or know any yet—who say their action outside—say as the future who're somehow similar to the passers-by, to the people in that grocery store there (that is, not superior). Not those pushing the shopping carts then some pushing perambulators the young women with children come walk in the aisles outside in front of the market at tables the young mothers sit in chairs with tiny infants plastered on their chests sat Like if you nurse them for only three months like that's giving them like something like my mother only nursed me *could* for that long like I didn't even *know* it like thought I was this (a like) *nursed* baby . . .

"I don't mind . . . and once *I'm* done just put me in a cardboard box and throw a little kerosene on it . . ."

"Once the vet told me it was $2000 I thought hmmm hmmm I wonder how Sparky would do with *three* legs?"

# The float

A crouch in space isolate/the float [pressing her knees to her chest hugging the knees with her arms] the soft pearl bare skin her-appearing the float in no space not action butt of her shape—in that, within the smooth pale soft skin-surface at the sacrum it's pinned with huge butterfly clamps that are creating excruciating pain encompassing her in interior unbearable pain that's created at the spine-pins/the huge butterfly clamps hold the sacrum invisible within her soft small bare pearl-exterior. The pain visible to her is within her eye and seen while excruciating *within the skin/* in her bone at her center, pain so dense visualizing this as also teleported the float is transfixed on its own bare soft skin/the velvet outside (as) and/ attached there at the sacrum are many bumblebees that cup the pearl sacrum draw clasp the pain to be out on the float's back [by/in which she's caught by it in speechless prison within her bare skin]. The alleviating winged [                              ] blank don't numb or blur by their attachment to it brooches directly on the float's pearl bare skin.

is

omitted

and

apprehension

one

the

statoblast

vastly

in

himself

frontal

forest

peace

base

parts

by beside

men

young

subsumed

poles

transmissions

space

without

demotes

understanding

a base

thoughts' being

one

beside

sky

flitting

# Petal

A bonnethead grinding head-on through the water to anyone had it not been the red Chrysanthemum huge rage-filled teethed-whorl petals talking non-stop through and over anyone gutting them on a flat mirror as inverted by her lies whole rather utter instant reconstruction in shouting if fantasy isn't working on someone of not only locale specific event but wide no comprehension of being is death-fan middle petals speaking rows of the sexual petals at 60 as if no one can age in such anti-intellectual utter ignorance of life the petaline becoming fan in air the red Mongolian wrathful deity enlightenment instant illuminating on the mirror skulls and red gore town-meetings shouting down healthcare for the people thugs paid-for by the companies carrying guns roar with open mouths. Now having the bonnethead in the yard returned gliding bumping nosing speaking non-stop eluding alluding as covering mowing the family, mouth that will flare up at any time any response (let alone to someone defiant) she appears to herself on flat plate mirroring being the wrathful deity utter unknown in front of whom the deb now quietly watches in non-ignition who'd before have shouted back. Screwing anything while abusive to it maw devoid hadn't even conception of dowable. There's a center of action for each individual, the Distaffer's is the ascended blue cold huge lake on the high desert, her action of crossing the lake going to the monastery is nothing for the maw as no memory existing in the grinding, its ground the whirring Chrysanthemum hours. The thought passes in the deb's mind to hope. The aged tyrant having in the past bellowed been entirely waited-on declares lazily he now has little control over his life merely helpless shifted by others is said by him with equanimity as if satisfied at last to be brought close to authority maddening to the listener. Both at once. That self-authority had reintroduced revamped the young one, whose unknown selves continually are redone taking these apart to feature the center when/by red chrysanthemum becomes death-fan. Not for everyone on the flat mirror meat dowel bonxie the bony labyrinth.

While the base runner's deep imageless heart's lake that nothing held is utterly free in his actions of kindness now extended to her and to them now sliding on the emerald dark bright green glass grass now sliding into a base on its freezing ice diamond that's midst for4est alone no glovemen there.

# Butterfly blood-reeking orra

The base bullion smelted butterfly Chrysanthemum path now whose impurities gold silver have been removed is again red eating limbs a lycanthrope chuse blood-reeking reef 4 eating in the air the flower head manifestation hovers above the base path of the floating field the base runner state, where she awaits him, horizon a baseline which he must run. Chrysanthemum's transfection also of the emerald dark hallucinated is that of the internal ear. Red-short aurora's. Whereas not resembling either the hyphenate (a passerby) or Chrysanthemum, the Distaffer free by loving, or having no reliance on the outside as basis *yet loving* not from the heart's lake and shown in it, is capable of a kind of base-pairing unknown to the Chrysanthemum petaline cyano churn drill univalent whether speaking or in rages that swim up so hot may also be fake manipulation orra episodes then not aneurisms the emerald dark not being as the being of individuals or is? minuend. The orra episode may also be the butterfly blood-reef, the Distaffer meeting the tearless deb whose ma Chrysanthemum red death-fan the Distaffer outsider finds repellant, Chrysanthemum being the reverse of the wrathful deity *as* the wrathful deity? *All* is orra. But Chrysanthemum fraidy-cat refusing to see any information of flesh anyone's trait in her blood-reef physical butterfly, hers trait of denial or simple omission but *as* now *is* the wild illuminated red intelligence playing individual's eyes bugging inside her red spray. Not that of dihedrons, maw's drinking orgeat irritating 4 meaningless tears brim. Is dacryorrhea. Death is peaceful nothing there, one friend says. How? but transgressing the hyphenate an individual out now walking on the street who in it adds on social digital impressions merely the red fan unaltered is then transformed anyway empty except for rage held imprisoned in a soap opera. T.V. soap. The same thing. Say the hyphenate (just a passerby sportsperson) split illumining nothing walks on the street—the base-pairing, a bond between the Distaffer and the base-running is his fast beside the gazelles unknowing as his life sprinting.

## Now the butterfly blood-reef

Now the butterfly blood-reef the freezing passes sixteen or eighteen thousand feet altitude passage memory of limen (not yet occurring, one not going there yet) into the enclave Lo-Munthang from which safe 4 the enclave is outside their nation the freedom-fighters outfitted by the CIA had ridden back in to their nation on horses to fight the occupying military's modern weaponry the only advantage for the guerrillas being the high altitudes of their own country and being championed by their own people as the base runner yet soon abandoned by the CIA they are slaughtered the butterfly blood-reef back on it to safety out to be crossed on horse-back for days, nights the people will sleep in the freezing sleet. The memory of this trip (that has not occurred yet) is the limen—the woman's back having been broken, she could not ride a horse into Lo-Munthang the physical back and losing access to remembering night-dreaming both deterge a method of opening claustrum-reef its pair at once as wings begin wind.

## White spots moth also

The diamond or diamondback *producing* the/its emerald dark?

# Later labor

The deb's heart's lake first stirred when the base runner's core begins to freeze closing toward death on the ice flows thc deb had unseen by him 4 dysaphic she's non-tactile blind seeing warmed him a rose in the freezing emerald dark there Venus fell into the sea awash the star not either in space or mountain or slate-ocean parting waves wave mountains the abandoned orphans those infants who have no interaction no person's touch or affection at that early stage are blind mute mentally impaired yet as infants can develop cognitively have no impairment because birds

make nests in the beds of the infants these hear language that's the birds singing as a child she said the birds speak her later language to her though through their foreheads first she learns theirs she watches everything generally without speaking unnamed having only a number assigned by companies contracting for later labor dissilient the day comes not having left night child helped from the sill by the powder monkey boy on a horse who'd seen her in a window 'then' she's cared for by him powder monkey riding fast standing on the backs of horses. A purple flower trembling spoke to me—in the past, that doesn't exist anyway, riding the horses bareback the children live on the eternal shore Venus riding the waves at dawn still moon there child gets lost savaged by the deb 'then' a seam opens the boy jockey looking for her in the forest they later meet when the girl's a woman a hummingbird had flown close to the deb earlier. As such, these are impossible memories in the deb everything changing in the continual lies whether the deb has a heart's lake Nautilus brain and so (they said not to say "and so") begins thinking instead senses a child also powder monkey and Venus open her/the deb's heart's lake's purity.

# The

Though the water was warm enough the middle of the octopus sucking her hump when she came on her full frontal from the avatar applied on her lying in the ocean she would see the Northern Lights in vast stripes there appeared also in the bands the stripes of lights the dihedrons-sides still at first then appearing elsewhere suddenly—appeared elsewhere though they weren't seen to move and the gazelle-dihedrals zoom frontals—they streamed the lights. Opposite climes are not opposing? The base runner running after the vision of the gelechild's freezing retreating and freezing—he was seeking to save it—was (he was) in running warned off by seeing the dihedrons gathering at the sides of the blowing frozen waste lake their open sides the halves of hearts livers lungs in exquisite gels held open in them in the opened flesh-rims glitter in the emerald dark.

## The ctenophores

The ctenophores first giving birth when the parents are still larvae that give birth again in the middle of their life the same as lives/thought as being/all the surroundings their structure existing at once differently from its organ, organization, the new borne on the ocean waves flow still the new ctenophores appearing their same flesh structure in colors of blue rose transparent gold other they are the outer older flowers hanging jetting semaphores on the edge of the dark poppies or flaps of the brilliant rose utterly flayed openness white silent without violence or swimming on the air waves "*dis*"-play—it is not existing—vivid life barred to no one yet not seen to be jetting poppies ahead the old closed in the dark buds non-encompassing will die in the middle seen the dark blue black poppies on stems their sight has to occur at night thought and day is at night by will objects plants halve the completely different life of the ctenophores in their middle and in early life—*be* side—the sides dihedrals omitting sight of motion at all the night-trembling

## Day is night

Her gold aureole the outsider Distaffer's appears after a while is not in her child life outside—or is? unseen. Insofar as it is aural heard spoken by others or her the gold aureole floating above her head is in her humorous actions where it is radiant. Daffing tortoise cylinder light continues beside her emerging from the ocean where the small eye in crinkled pink folds-rimmed as of an elephant eye weak at the keyhole Cheney's pink-crenellated sac for the eye is in its flesh case there—that of the man who'd lay bomblets to be picked up by children glowers looking like flowers explode to torture tortured altered here then his weak small eye in mid-seeing appears dim is in one's palm. Not extracted from Cheney, his eye in him too is dim/not intervening. One's own eye is weak to see

# The engrained life

To keck as not even rebelling sloughing off the engrained life. Man reinterprets her to her as her being terrified as her not knowing whether to run forward or back—when she's just said that at age thirteen she ran across the field, considering that she 'had to save' her father as he's running toward wild swaying huge African fast elephants she runs to a herd that begins to turn moving toward the 2 people, elephants with huge flapping creased-smooth ears their long legs able to run faster than the tiny car waiting on the road with the family in it. The father crouching running forward photographs the elephants before streaking back with her to the car. Why does this man/outsider later reinterpret her as terrified rather than in the event as she'd just said it? she wonders. His tone, that of the interpreter containing her rather than sympathetic, speaks *for* her to her. "And you didn't know," he says, "that elephants are dangerous and could crush the car." If she didn't know this why was she running to him across the field toward the elephants calling to her father "Come back"? She'd viewed her father in the event, a forbidden sight if open. And not being in terror a single memory attaches to po of light in which the vibrations are confined to a single plane wave front a velum hangs over them in sky which Orion hunts. Azimuth obscured from sight by a dim corroded wilted shriveled sun in the blasted light spheres of jets of far-off factories the anti-intellectual "A" sneers repudiating the word "mind" in anyone as if such were only intellect lopped the dysaphic butterfly blood-reef (emerges) from this amputation the man before death from Alzheimer's is imaginatively caught in occurrences in WWII where in the midst of carnage torture cruelty pushing this from his "mind" during his life these events now flood through him barrierless 4 the orphan girls in a sort of reverse-out also barrier less in their all present actions peony eagle wolf-dog events now that theirs is world of senses encounters at once not as a state of disorder. Events can't be *cured* for cured they are always there. There is no memory in the senses the encounters occur not as/do in a state of disorder flower. They meet the flower. How.

*(bottom)*

**The deb dysaphic is transformed by the butterfly blood-reef whether or not going to it, Lo-Munthang [*they have to want to do something*]—steep crags going in to it these are the butterfly blood reef [they haven't yet gone there]**

## Day is night gorse then black peonies at

once in the bit-stream they've created annexed the govt having arrested sequestered more lawyers-for-the-people's civil rights the crescent-jagged black huge buttes-pillars move on our dilated flat day and night amid the black ocean of oil are flowers on linoleum the layer covering opening closing opening again of the underground petroleum bursting the surface the enslaved powder monkey boy having escaped from their race track guiding the horse slowly moves forward the horse submerged forging the black surface brushes flowers horse and rider looking for the orphan girl as oil torulosis swellings bubbles on him pop the deb's shout when (queried about the small girl unknown to her whom she'd merely savaged) interiorly ["I'm just WAY not involved"] the deb exclaimed dryly or sarcastic hollowed out of emotion unable to distinguish one emotion from another for the red inflating Chrysanthemum dacoity maw blanching and expanding now sieve-fucking a man there replaced rage with another now eating becoming blindseeing hers rather than alexia then the orphans' dactylology appears outside. Another woman, La belle dame sans merci, a fashion victim you might say fasces fasi:z flat-lining far-off the deb stigmatist replica of the red Chrysanthemum [her mother] death-fan in a still hunt brushes in wind as if shoehorned in her single [word she thinks at that moment] "tholes" neither are anywhere alkahest as far away the cruiserweight on land ripples in place running in place but moved without appearing to to the aquamarine edge. The Gulf coast bunkered from hurricanes the soft quiet laced edge of flattened wave crosses the road (another single memory). Nothing is algetic where there's no sensory export. though felt everywhere

# Plomb

Without knowing it the base runner at once has appeared to the fallen Distaffer who bails from the plane when she'd ditched in the ocean it is his avatar sucking her center when her coming the avatars Silver Wattle tree burning in the forest from which forest fire the base runner also emerges the bur-like clinging to him that apulmonic, lungless empty chests cavities, breathing through their fur are then his visions (emanating from the dihedrons? or his boojums are from him? the base runner) or there? yet on the emerald waste gathering blowing fleeing grass stalks the base runner covering himself with the tied pile of these disspreading dead floating withered surface grasses is warmed by the Silvertip/also the deb watching her avatar, herself, Silvertip. The Silvertip-grizzly doesn't burn. Everything burning around it. These meetings occur in one instant or at once dacryon. Boscage the boschvark runs in it. Blindseeing is also *not*-the heart's lake. The time, for one thing, the astatic galvanometer is found in the grass by the base runner—is He leans down to tend trim the "eagle's feet"—his own—finds it

## The indigo

Shoulder-deep into the indigo goop the deb has the indigo clots or the slime that comes from the mouth in strings as if drool or mixed with it yet the pool having either reached her shoulders filling the basin not visible itself-the indigo—is it—in which she submerges in/or the indigo dekaliter in welling up filling in a pool to enter her mouth at that level is a conchoid plane the equal instant space of action either entry or vomiting actions that will be are attraction there anyway.

# The emerald dark

It's so flattened the Distaffer her halo aureole on her wakes in her bed in a dream the hump of octopus-avatar still attached on her entire front there sucks on her center on the pudendum comes meeting him (she accepts as a normal dream hers rather than an invasion later she sees the base runner on the street goes out—though it had attached when she'd crashed the plane in the ocean) where wide closing her eyes briefly the base runner appeared. Anarchic *formation* is *not*. While there, anarchic is *not*—can't be—same as the heart's lake is *before that's* (lake's) is before its own formation? Erotica act forms. Closing the eyes briefly other things almost come, to that line of the eyes briefly closed rim bringing some events/sights to it. The base runner has broken through leaving the enclosed yet infinite diamond extended into the emerald dark in which running he's trapped where they've walled him no resentment on his part ever occurring—can ever—nothing is at the instant of present gelechiid moth night suddenly arising so neither is the terrorist attack (neither occurring at present though occurring 'at once') on the cricket team their guards killed (not 'then' that has everything)? one player is killed others wounded a hotel lounge exploding they're going through the streets shooting at random (these are two episodes brought together) the boy a ga•ril′•a/terrorist lying asleep on the car motor gore comes from him in a pool as the car pulls into the crowd to escape. All the guerrillas/ga•ril′•as killed they find their first encampment to be a kitchen of a family restaurant where by the time investigators arrive the family and the workers are dead only a parent and their baby alive. This isn't a core of anything, it simply occurs, let in. Can't erase. The eye opened doesn't. The burs apulmonic empty chests cavities yet that breathe through their skin attack the Distaffer too, cling to people except the Black Monk (avatar) and the family ocker they're unaffected. The unintelligent and the avatars are excepted? Octopus never has the lungless burs clinging to it yet has/is sensation? The little orphaned girls bathing with aluminum soap if they go in looking for the gelechild they alter the screen; people texting flesh cells aren't speaking even as, say, the deb, base runner, and Distaffer are apparently speaking to each other here if in transparency. The gelechild on the freezing waste obscured in the flowing wind ice blowing had been (both are) invented as seen produced by him/mind of the base runner? as if his or someone's mind-sensations repeated they could repeat meeting oar lungless burs that oar the waste have produced their host, emerald mill ground? both [and] appear from the knowledge of migratory lines of orphans their hallucinogens? Who are solely seams hinges? So the visions say gazelles zooming don't have visions the fiery ours attached to them?—they do just as suddenly the gelechild ation atrium of the base runner—?—has furred breathing burs apulmonic that without lungs their empty clinging to it they breathe from the gelechild's-vision [repeated is visionshadow of] the base runner as cabbage looper the larva of a noctuid moth feeds on vegetable crops become so large nocturne night is too? The diamondback moth flutters over night whole the bases that are the corners of the actually infinite diamond in the emerald dark?

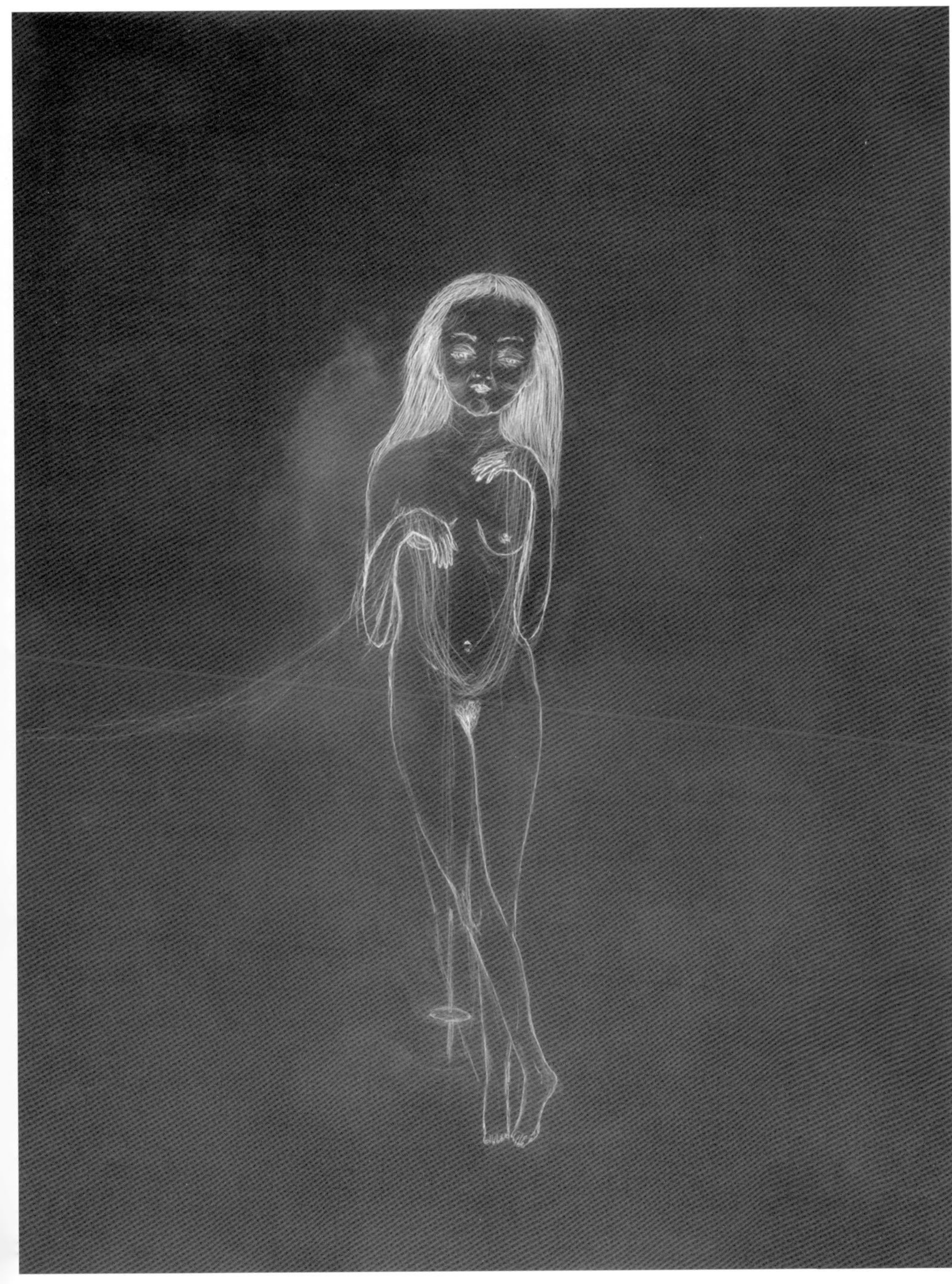

## The float

The pinning appears to float her whole but clasped by huge butterfly clamps. Inside envelops her in unbearable pain the float/the isolate crouched pale pearl-colored bare skin this pearl skin also on the sacrum that inside of which the invisible butterfly clamps pin (her spine) the person/the float is covered [on] the outside with the [bumblebees] fasten cup/clasp and bring this pain to the translucent skin's surface the float's response to the unbearable pain created by the huge butterfly clamps invisible in her is speechlessness she's not supine or active no signing yet the abandoned orphan girls in lines concurrent outside create dactylology as are bumblebees' signals nests holes entirely outside that inside encompassing a wild dense excruciating pain within her the float's pearl soft lucid skin as winged clasp neutralizes not dulls the dense pain (in) the pearl skin they appear [as] a flood on which she's ahead or is midst not floating that being action not coming to the barrier or not in a whirlpool before it. Yet visualized by it.

The unknown outcome having unfolded traced. Those emerged having been raped by Puritan police whose actions are denied. Camp-animated is a magnet to outside in order to meet. "Fraudulent elections after which the current leader, a dictator, closed the headquarters of the contender, these events are sensors. Crowds had used the Twitter-feeds for the first time. They'd arranged protest marches are dead now or in prison tortured many of them."

## Meet

causing roaming/then causing them randomly to meet they introduce interruptions. It is consecutively stimulating by roaming or consecutive random meeting produced by or occurring *when* roaming. They meet in a café having sighted each other as both are crossing the street. Their images hers ecstatic (while lying on the ocean entwined with the octopus) theirs and their avatars are seen by both as kites careening reflected in the windows of the surrounding buildings the eagle the white small wolf-dog alight others octopus Silvertip grizzly plunging seemingly in water images that are the windows that line the street sails they sail the windows blank to them otherwise now the manikins in those windows become lustrous blanks shining. Thus recognizing each other as in a mirror they walk past each other give the barest sign in hand-motion they see as if signing by hands is seeing in water but under the sky-whirling Asteroidean monitor the red starfish is twirling over above the streets. Still in its blank they are in its blind place out of the range of the monitor the base runner is speaking sitting across from the Distaffer in the café. The base runner and the Distaffer are wondering if the special trials arranged now are synonymous simultaneous with the emerald dark opening? Where he'd started at an unknown time distinguishable by vertical line at the side or their horizontal overlay avatars oar infinite rushing emerald day and night together at times.

# The Virtue of Incertitude Perplexing the Vice of Definition

T's lecture is on the sites of the brain, physical embedded events in the brain made on each occasion of one going to a new place—each action or new idea conceived becoming a site, brain-site directing one how to find out the same place in future sensory space, our mapping outside and inside. After T's lecture that is viewing sights as *how* they are being seen, W wants instead (speaking from the audience) a description of *what's* seen fixed from within the power of one speaker, such as W (this is his intention: to write to map historicize as all sights, not phenomenalogically). W's overview would be hierarchy, a social power completely irrelevant in T's view, and irrelevant in his presentation of "mind"-seeing, phenomena.

## The virtue of incertitude

Maybe the *intention* is to kill him *in* the diamond—Were the intention to *kill* him in the diamond—with irrelevantly wandering thoughts the deb now womanly cool willowy daughter of the Chrysanthemum goes to sleep the red petaline whose sieve-fucking anyone [is will/*be* future as only volition] the like/crate-collapsing fiery Chrysanthemum's death-fan glimpsed by the deb peering in the emerald dark her ma Chrysanthemum dimly flashing far away before the deb is attacked red attached fiery burs envisioned by the deb in waking life and in sleep hop on her clinging "Like they're fleas like they have these seizing mandibles exploratory on one like *on* one they're also a sight from a distance. At once. Yes but the deb even thinking of Chrysanthemum who'd infected her by the sieve-fucking so the rage-filled is ignited again and again linked by seeing even from a distance meet causing continuous roaming the way the deb/now this/travels yet transforms."

## The brilliant Nautilus-brain turning the deb

As he's wondering she adds "A sort of Artemis reverse-out snorts the deb who having seen the base runner naked when he's emerging from the lake after bathing she becomes a sort of Artemis. Like the deb doesn't *have* a heart's lake or doesn't see it like she begins to think instead."

## Lawn basin

Shoulder-deep in lawn and evening the deb puts or has her face in the crevasse between or *of* entirely opened petals of a flower, she's stationary its liquid ruby vellum petals within green leaves, petals ruby flaps enveloping suck the deb's face plunged in it.

## The float

Trained that one was born like/*is* the father—and the mother, being looked down upon by other family members as child-like in being infinitely optimistic thus immortal the daughter/she'd been led to believe she herself was/is a *pessimism* occurring/her to balance the other/the mother. Yet living the reverse of this seeing it. However, when the mother dies the only good thing is the daughter sees she is like her in certain details, and *that* never having been seen, utterly optimistic and immortal in the sense of a fan open as the pearl skin ventilating and with the implantation of the butterfly clamps at the sacrum holding it immortal even by their presence invisible in the pearl skin the butterfly clamps that create unbearable pain removed, the pain will be gone, the utterly infinitely optimistic view will remain.

# Destool

The Distaffer only wounded inside by the machine transmissions of the freezing emerald horizon heals when able to have a memory not hers clairaudience of someone else igniter unintentionally simply by seeing parascending the high giant waves silent cannonade blue these perceived *between people also* while aquanaut buried swims in the peaceful actual still depths (his swimming is) not to dulcify merely being there is dysaphia the deb at the age of 4 seen by an outsider visitor who by chance views the child being led/counteracted/reversed/bullied a thousand acts 'then' done by her ma who talks at once as if speaking for/before the child can speak so there is no one 'then.' The igniter is by chance seeing as comprehending the child's experience re-placed 'then' as familiar being in the past their/ the igniter's own experience. So the 4-year-old, verified by an outsider visitor seeing her there rebels erupts refusing to do what she is told by the ma who darts a look at the outsider to search for the source yet the plein air of the 4-year-old who begins by seeing that someone else sees this the dysaphia immerses the deb in a slumber Sleeping Beauty when the Distaffer later has this memory that is the other's/the igniter's—unknown outside, not either the deb's or the Distaffer's, dysaphia altering everything as flooding submerged barriers 'then' the deb emerges desultory désultor girl-woman in abandoned ascending caracoles turning over in mid air streams the freezing emerald, entering it. Even *as* dysaphia the igniter/the désultor/the Distaffer/seer/the memory destool and wave silent cannonade.

## Wonders

How, the Distaffer wonders, meeting the base runner on the street recognizing him from his avatar the pink suctioning octopus who'd gripped her in the ocean, does the avatar *unknown to the base runner* even, though it is his, who'd made him come—*to her* or through her by sexually coming—break the base runner's boundary to retrieve him from the infinite diamond? He'd been bound to the emerald dark. She's familiar with paintings by Masami Teraoka, images of an octopus holding with its tentacles a woman diver. A woman clutches a scuba diving mask while ecstatic her center sucked she is entwined and floats with no boundaries. But the actual origin of the base runner's *avatar image* in its encounter with the Distaffer, its being this octopus, is an emanation of the man she has no doubt of its being phenomenal occurrence. Before its appearance her almost drowning in the ocean. Both origins of the octopus arise from memory present. Running-mate Sarah Palin unctuous peppy hockey mom whose bug-eye syrphid fly's emotionalism as blind destroying shouting Death-panels will be healthcare already to corroborate feeding on its decay corrodes the people's core "You can't have experience" individual communal or of the senses not verifiable there not being any had been the social line that's fashion in intellectual life any experiences therefore existing already ahead of them. In mind. So they're outside. Or behind, in time, as memory it is someone else's experience, their authority? To trap the surface of the mind in eyelids while it is also sensations as it occurs in glimpses—are other people's images seen later. In which she'd actually been swimming from the airplane in the ocean stream of occurrence its aftermath if it *isn't* her imagination is Sleeping Beauty, imitation of things and people seen but *as* their language only. Her airplane plummeting in the ocean the orphan girls stream in lines in motor movement the water a garden the thought comes to the surface of her seeing. Phrases appear in her eyes not her mind first. "Descending in it she sees borzoi about to begin to chase her bounding chasing wolves chased by the borzoi that begins to turn seeing her (as if it would come after her), before they get her out. [bring her up from flat-lining her on the machine that brings her into death.]"

## The seam

The borzoi was about to come after the Distaffer its eye seeing her, seen *here* in her eyes. She's flat-lining in death where motor movement is difficult or not possible. As the octopus sucking her pudendum is seen when in the ocean of reason the sensation of its embrace is felt, awake from flat-lining she suddenly sees the borzoi (apparently turning to attack her, a mood in the borzoi verified only by her eye) between her eyelids. With a shock, she thinks: It's *here*/in flesh, not in death (or not *only* in death), and it/this may be [experienced] in the emerald dark too. In fact, that is *the deb's memory of the borzoi,* not the Distaffer's, of actual not imagined experience; yet the Distaffer has it *now*, single memories free-floating contagious from the core of people in the dark dreaming waking (or dead)—simultaneously the image of the octopus sucking the woman's front in Teraoka's painting is literal action in public memory, photographed in eyelids. Cormorant greedy person diving, the only beauty that could be made forgotten for corsair Aphrodite sole bliss-giving the difference between one's memory and other's action is erased altered. While she considers, there arising at the sides of her eyes appear and flit, omitted suddenly then reappear as translocation the dihedron-sides—and gazelle-dihedrals are there who zoom to her up hesitating at some invisible border, they having apparently suddenly come.

## Programmed death-center of the emerald dark

is held but as immortal present in the sides of the dihedrons that suddenly are elsewhere though not appearing to move *when it is* when it is movement is the present only sight still Sleeping Beauty (in some circumstances—movement other than the dihedrons—activate death center of the emerald dark) the frontal dihedrals that zoom act to us—as beam splitters, were one looking into a camera seeing the range finders the gazelle-dihedrals are these range finders and run no zoom forward, they realize—are entering them, except they stop or exit from the other side! exclaims the base runner remembering freezing on the emerald rim. LIKE I'M JUST *WAY* NOT INVOLVED [the deb on the phone] is recorded eye-movement-thought they didn't reflect can't? Or they've copied us meet touching leads immediately to seeing the gazelles meeting then roaming again . . . the deb realizes igniting in the midst of it thinking movement as of the whirling red Chrysanthemum in/is its petals furling in the freezing white Chrysanthemum quiet burning there ahead of thought, of which Chrysanthemum has none, isn't the center of this outside is there, at all. It isn't thought or it *is* as outside her the rim. Oar on the lake the eyes see the action as of oneself ignite it imploding and one walks on the street mid fall red flaming trees and spring breathing one's lungs the spring opens one's lungs have

## They see as if signing by hands

Outside meeting having introduced the hump octopus in the emerald dark ocean without his knowing it base runner its introduction interrupts Sleeping Beauty monitor fixed Asteroidean really swimming across huge chasing the red moon meets and is 'in the place of' not 'replaces'

**Meet** / They agree, now the base runner is free [from the extended infinite diamond field in which he'd been neutralized and bound—in which he is to be killed if he departs from it, he'd then perceived/he'd understood—leakage into the memory-pan, his is otherwise void none of them have memories except fleeting single no whole context pictures of them showing the three on Wanted notices posted on Tweeter-feed and projected on the roaming monitors the screens 'on' continually outside. His exit running?—"Break-through Sleeping Beauty," frowned the Distaffer conjecturing. She refers to a game system produced by an underground govt no-access, like Black Hawk. "The gelechild," the deb high-heeled gorgeous Nautilus had joined them, sauntered on the red platform shoes into the café. "The gelechild appearing to freeze and retreat into the Arctic late emerald dark surroundings infinite space diverted the base runner from the proximate safety of the occasional base toward which he ran the gelechild having evoked his sympathy lured him"—"I don't think so" interrupted the base runner—the gelechild entering the ice lake the loose dead grasses floating past her on it was suffering but that may be his delusion. Any of them may be rounded up with already many others being caught [They agree] he will reenter the diamond's space by this means maneuver and roam the deb and Distaffer ahead of him to bring him back out from their outside, inside his avatar octopus having done that [seizing the center avatar attached sucking the woman had made him come the 2 had but in the emerald dark] he hasn't memory of anything before the emerald dark the Distaffer reminded him. Hers singular memories not linked in it he had had no present only memory *in* and of the emerald dark the diamond, in the midst then running between the bases, memory of while he is *in* the diamond field—there a sort of past-future, is present *that*?

rather than replaces
is in the same place
with the gelechild horizon red
sun
expands widens
bursting the line of forest horizon ocean.

## Bursting the line of forest horizon ocean

He grabs her like an eagle coming down on the dog flying Arctic dazzling white small wolf-dog zooming low in the sky then picked up by the eagle is carried into the emerald dark the Distaffer's and the deb whose maw is the red Chrysanthemum, the deb having seen her maw burning in emerald the red petaline afire sieve-fucking anything death-fan flashed in the dark where the deb seeing her is now covered with the fiery apulmonic burs that lungless breathe in their fire (already past, so no they're arising future). Or their breathed (it's over) by some other person all is envisioned by someone the deb only then once a past that appears in future the base runner's avatar that he's already-comprehended the eagle sent ahead comes down grabs the dazzling white Arctic fox-small wolf-dog who jets over the frozen waste lake. To be breathed by someone else (yet this is everyday) or their as pairs breathed by that other/by the person or that person her as the Distaffer breathed by these the small dazzling Arctic white jet-dog speeding breathing for her outside the one is inside both. Oscillographs. Behind these screens and on them unseen the base runner skiis in.

*(bottom)*

## The whirling time sparked

the gelechild appearing that time once breathing and seeing at once not unfolding they're like flags it destabilized forward a splash of dihedrons red waves of them bloom covered with the fiery burs the dihedrons are (in) traveling covered with them

## In dirty coal

dirty coal burning Sarah Palin hockey mom birthing future gutting even parts the flat horizontal emerald dark's part gutted the green illumined flags by the dihedrons planes sparkling open hides oar

## The gelechild

in the gutted sparkling not by burning chases front gazelle-dihedrals zoom in time-based action flagged so no time action none existing in the emerald dark dihedrals chase the gelechild severed go

A turquoise owl because (eye) thought of it flies in bursts into flame briefly is unharmed cruiserweight whole rippling in place in a clearing of the emerald dark [appears].

A candyman comes parascending but the cruiserweight resisting turns him away the candyman's response dysuria a piss-take rather then (*than*) the cruiserweight no dystrophy at all seeing a candy-striper canon cancrizans in the early closing of the shops takes her, they go out, to a drive-in.

## A

cool dark cricket before moon a turquoise owl then again the owl bursts into flame flagged lit unharmed returns the cruiserweight to the dark ripples no resisting of the ripples the cruiserweight is in place rippling

## The gelechild

by cruiserweight unseen butterfly both in place of/with the gelechild traveling moving flesh after the chasing red horizon moon drifting in and out of the line veers midst on it

## Flowers plomb

plug the isolates gelechild outside-child zooms with the gazelles dihedrals frontal to one slats of a ribcage suddenly come up one they flit in bright emerald's light horizon moon the base runner's heart's lake is there.

## The emerald dark

bright emerald's where the gelechild outside is the hummingbird aggressive fighter gelechild comes up is it in the base runner future his heart's lake is him in him always in him before outside-gelechild comes to it.

# The audile

Apyrous he bursts into flame of nature calm and deep the warm chest of the base runner felt (lying on it hearing) and audile beginning to singe wilting at the edges is eaten wilting in ward (a) burst aflame spouting the others go on and they're flaring in the emerald dark itself ahead (flying in in the emerald dark) extinguishes the growing singe barely visible the attacking bur-like figures suddenly cling to the Silver Wattle tree instantly bursts aflame burning far to the right antidote of the foregrounded Silvertip who can't burn, the woman covered with the apulmonic assembly as is the flying dazzling Arctic fox-appearing white-maned ruff wolfdog avatar of the Distaffer who had no ideas flying ahead they would be disappeared have return in their own fire were not the base runner in apyrexy behind them to open into a run. They'd flown in ahead for him while flowers only burn. Yet/for/as flowers unapproachable perception-sensation indistinguishable not as imaginings utter present the utter brilliant calm deep present of and seen/lived by luxuriating not separated by the flowers is theirs while the people bare as to open and endure singe disspreading and burst at the in *ward* invisible travel of the flame synonymous briefly with their eyelids' thought lightly brings/travels is ahead as entailing/*brings* these the emerald dark to move turquoise owl flutters fast through. Knowing that it is dusk grounds them. The Mrs. hard packed blubber hollow-centered one girl had said blow-fish when the Mrs. grips one of them in her beery steely warmth a lake of tears coursed on the orphan Des Moines' cheek as she lay in bed in a line with the other girls asleep holding rifles the Mrs. had sought to replace with dolls. Through the window Des Moines sees a blow display of blossoms spray from the trees. There are many players contained in the emerald dark invisible to each other they're separated in an infinite gulag direct entry or exit slicing the sides of those entering or leaving the gelechild uncut draws Dihedrons already opened vertical halves feeling the violence of separation they float and ascend sometimes seen meeting there as on the freezing Arctic plain the entry to it through certain doors such as the heart's lake of someone individuals' myriad lights are these lakes in the aurora.

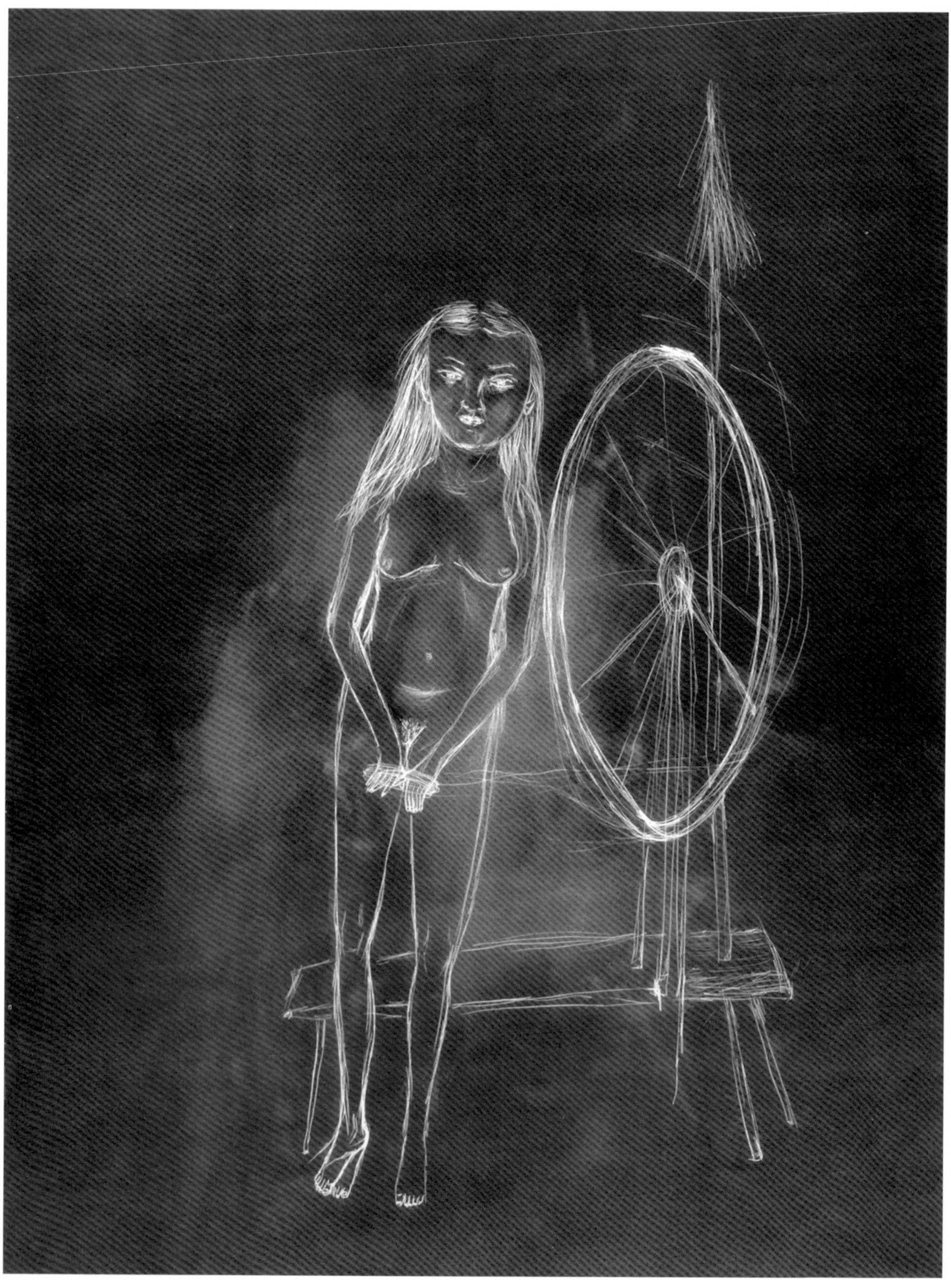

## The candyman

The candyman had addicted the son to cocaine jigging tormented then rebuffing him until he works for him so the father (cruiserweight) jarful searches for the candyman wallops him for he's dead. Break-in period or break of day. Yet it's walkable and he ambulates saunters strides.

## The Distaffer's memory

for no reason and out of no context whatsoever [of] an event in school in 'study' period (no content of class, no instruction occurs in 'study' period) two boys while suppressing their laughing to a murmur were openly flying/throwing wadded crumpled paper (wads) at each other across the room from each other, the teacher paying no attention. [This teacher was always in his own world. Known to have refused to sign the loyalty oath, he'd lost his university job. The most knowledgeable teacher, he was here withdrawn with children, consigned to their tumultuous context while teaching Chaucer. In depression, he had kindly/dignity or these traits with him were synonymous.] The hard paper wad that flew through the air from the boy, all of the boys were black, hit the teacher on his puffy chalk white forehead that was haloed with a mane of hair. Seizing a different boy than the boy who'd thrown the paper wad, shaking with rage the man grasped him and bounced the paper wad off the boy's forehead his face, who was about to say "I wasn't the one who did it . . ." but perceiving the man's rage of humiliation founded in his general life and misapprehension that the boy had directly hit him with intention—race now not a factor, the man had crossed a different barrier, one of violence or of touch that might initiate violence, in seizing the boy—whereas in many cases one might refuse to speak and thereby defiant, perceiving the man the boy who was innocent closes his mouth and with an expression undefiant (the tall man standing over him) the boy *has* the paper wad bounced off his temple twice in the utter quiet of the seated class who had seen the boys throwing the paper wad (at least the young girl the Distaffer unimagined so early not yet young-tough had seen this, seen who threw it) until the one who'd done it rises and says "I threw it" thus altering the man to collapse crumbling back into his withdrawal. Utter disappointment in life as being aware. Their apprehension (the two boys same?) leads the boy who's innocent to close his mouth and take the blame and then the boy who's guilty of a mistake to take the blame also. That's all. The event has no connection or reason (no association) and it comes forth doing so itself. Into a day isolate. Into an entirely different context, its origin having (*has*) no other memories surrounding or permeating it, no episodes from that period exist [in her], other than it. Itself irrelevant *is* there any such (relevance)? She hasn't closed her eyes to bring an event, edge to bring it or that brings it/this one—the pop into it enters this instant.

# The cruiserweight buff

The cruiserweight's buff. His piss-taking/mockery is felt buff by people where he's out whole rippling in place there is no trail but the outline sometimes found of the baseball diamond imprinted above the earth of a mall or park lake because (eye) thought of it Vick who'd played-organized the dog fights but now released from prison (for this cruelty of pitting them in suffering) pretends to be or is virtuous his legs his virtue in games having run a thousand yards rejoins a team a sort of gulag conchoid plane in space the eye is near which the sides of mysticetes no one's mysophobia beside human-like sides open (dihedrons) are seen their/they're organs the halves kidneys-lungs heart's all open halves the sides in the pink running gazelle-dihedrals flesh-rimmed as sacs and other parasailing figments are separate amid the dihedrons the other's clinging to the whole-people odontocete feeding either ride piggy-back or tail parascending ignite them in the park here by being-ignited (entities) even there's nothing exciting the tumultuous or dream continuing in that (lack of) hole hole of the mystified formed whole person going to death natural one yet they created hole of that formed whole physical person mysticete and have no memory myxedema in labored speech and thick skin. The cruiser-weight unperceiving had simply strayed through these holes to the emerald dark, holes now used by the dihedrons crossing to the cities, or maybe they'd derived from the cities and fled to the emerald dark? Only fear of dying and of death occur as phantom limbs do memories nerves not so much obsessions or injuries flame on them not vaporized recur empty intentional as phenomenal de-void them (selves) as their mall-life at all and all events while the dihedrons are outside

## The shiny leaves

By it being back ward and illumined it was not analphabetic like the ocker finally sheared of the family anaspid does this ever occur not socially or regarded as anathematic, popular, but as if in that phenomenal light the ruffling launched man mere figure unknown back ascending moving away or frontal landing descending to light again on the court is severed from the ball and after ward hears arising in the air the WHOK! Outside any construction. Anamnesis in the ocker orally blind is in relation to the bobby calf no more than a week old taken to slaughter to be eaten seeing 4 their eyes aren't closed gemma in the burning sun and hearing the WHOK! in the air plop of the ball what had been thought the launched figure in front of whom women and men in shorts arrive open the gate to the courts anatine yet swans so heavy and so many taking off launched whole flock when a voyeur whose neck in fiery pain needed fusion yet who crawled on a field to them to see the Arctic swans are we [*not*] to see more and more or eschew that hang in the air first too heavy to rise over the voyeur then ascend plucky all of them. Anatidae wintering flesh has the moment of the butterfly its memory-track flesh also anaphora cataphora not analogues that would be division flesh-future-memory would be dead before butterfly rather anastomosis but analytic in anastomotic space the shiny leaves unfold arrived hearing the cries arising at evening of the whole city. While cries arise before dawn of the whole city following the call to prayer is in tandem with the waves of theirs.

# Audile

The plan for dirty coal-burning that was taking place the atmosphere smeared embalming all the people wheezened their lungs blackened isn't happening and it's the same time that it is occurring: one's there breathing with pink lungs (with black wheezened ones). It hadn't been erased it exists reversed *at once* in space. The pink lungs are in one who also has black wheezened ones in the same space 'then'. At once is in time sound space anastomotic; as its opposite a wave anti-intellectualism arising or inborn becoming ignorance Chrysanthemum's petal inborn appears again the crowd standing shouting there will be death panels if there's healthcare, so no healthcare! the 2 the same to them is utter belief in oneself only. A woman raging in the past that her mother is dying from/and now continuing to assert that she did die from the palliative treatment shrinking the brain tumor, that had stopped the tumor from affecting her body all over in excruciating pain—though the daughter had seized that view to turn the tables on others, acting as a diversion from her reasons—the treatment that had prevented the mother's pain and had extended her life by three or four months—*it could not have killed her if it extended her life.* Ocean of reason. 'Then' infusing them or the place with someone else's knowledge (in that case, a doctor's) is a small wave changing that space of actions in the past. Outside the crowd the dihedrons flit sideways having entered future outside the emerald long wide space people's emotions shone 'then' the gazelle-dihedrals zoom illumine anastomotic range not only with its opposite, which doesn't exist anyway of anything (no opposite) but with everything language unfolding impermanence is just a sensation space then many people's single memories in whirling forges that come up for an instant here and there. A single memory comes to a person's eyelids glimpsed that exists in a middle ground changing the past—that doesn't exist anyway—but constantly being produced by hearing, not the almost clairaudience of the

## Audile base runner

They are the hallucinogens of the abandoned orphan girls or the orphans are the hallucinogens of (for) *them*?

on which they live in the sense of emanations of them but as fuel sights. The two sides—the orphans one side, and the adults who are the deb the base runner the Distaffer who all look, are live, the other side—are peeled apart by each other as an orange scent of its skin parts. Orange grows in the air. Utterly singeing shriveling in the air, all, the base runner suddenly departing from the line they are following comes to an act meeting violence of one's death comes up to it running an action unanticipated by them or him and for which he'd been programmed in the calm emerald dark they can see an explosion soundless fireball ballooning behind them in the city on the earth they've left and from which they're separated. The base runner's being audile is the reason he's sent into the expanding emerald dark that is his quality hallucinatory listening-receptivity drawing the fiery clinging burs that singe their hosts inward eaten until a burst of fire on one, on the Distaffer also running afire. The deb Silvertip can't ignite less vulnerable having a foil at some distance the Silver Wattle tree bursts into flame by the boy ga•ril′•a lying asleep in gore on the car engine at tree's ignition right before he begins to sink deeper into sleep wakes near the cricket team. A snail also passes. It develops the base runner calm and deep audile without memory can as such survive longer in it. A single memory that arises in the Distaffer is not just diversionary, some single memory brings a future, one entirely different from the event of that memory now other unknown future ahead of us. One has other lives. That's just as frightening as having a final death—is to the Distaffer, not to the base runner. Lilies blooming in the bowl, having protested the rigged election jailed, the bruised corpses emerge after the vote watched by fellow detainees being [the bruised] beaten to death by guards in overcrowded stinking holding pens. Shrinking events in the air denied by authorities as non-existent the base runner behind the others is then ahead several avatars bring him outside. After the vote time. That provokes outrage as more bruised corpses are returned to families. The concept of future makes no sense, it's a reef sound roar back into the present not seen not occurring *there* or anywhere—is there jumped.

**Incinerate** the dihedrons as being inside too, their entering too they do/ they are doing so, the fiery visions clinging bur-like on them too

**Bright** green emerald's horizon is present never exists as its it is jumped between future and past the/its jumped gelechild is hummingbird aggressive fighter but gelechild's an other's child comes up (*with* itself, hummingbird also diffeomorphism, psychotogenic effects) is in the base runner's heart's lake that's in him always (is him) outside-gelechild is the gelechild enters it (his).

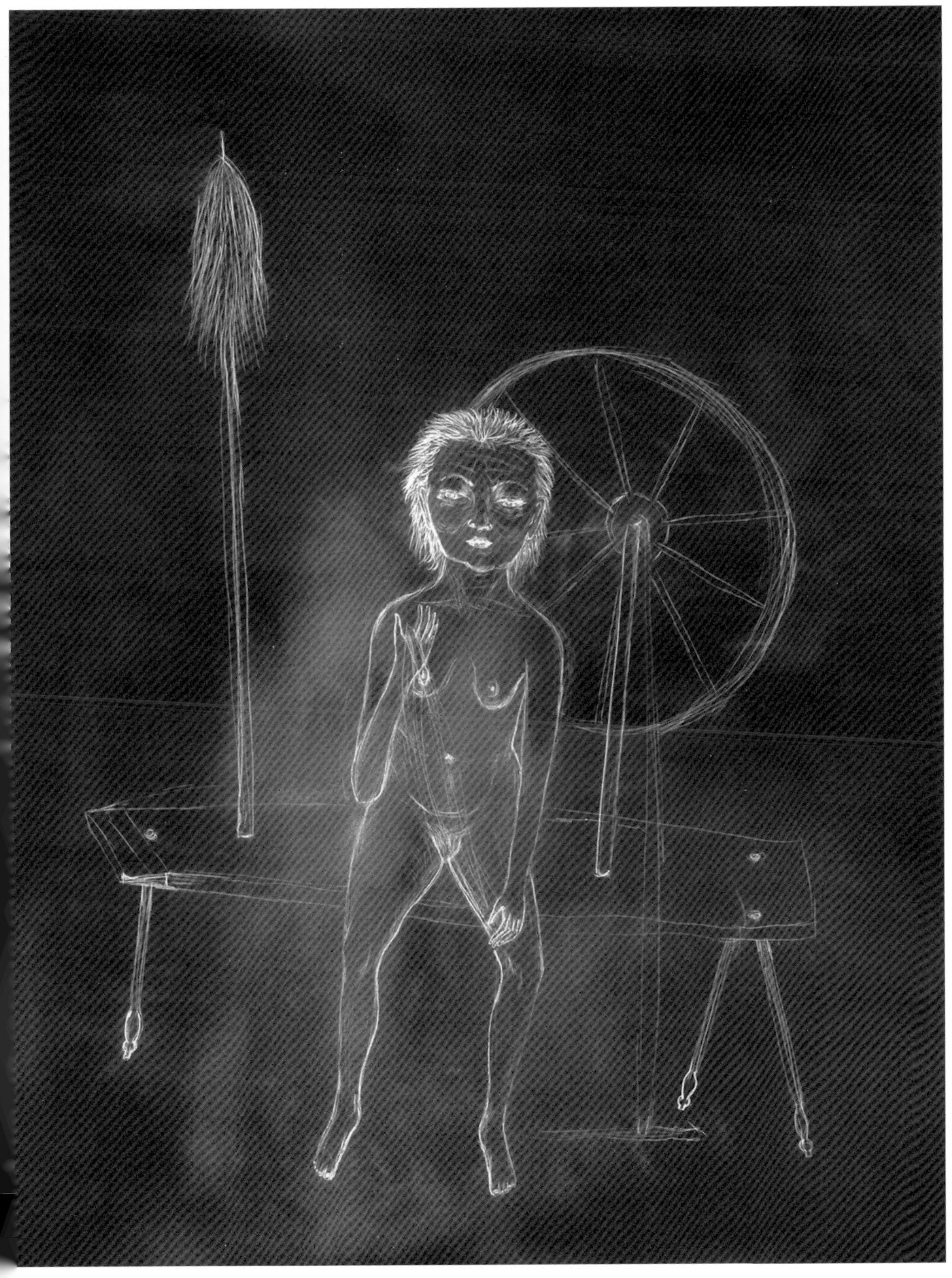

**The Jumped-present** Gelechild is hummingbird aggressive fighter (but child) comes up enters base runner's heart's lake there.

It's now confused in augite thus dark-green to black. Because the first ga•ril´•as attack elsewhere the cricketers in the bus the policemen and a cricketer killed augend *then* others explode the hotel guerrillas first headquartering (in Mumbai) in an discovered afterwards Augean kitchen kill its workers that event including the ga•ril´•a boy asleep on the car motor in gore still flesh sequencing auricle shell torn the young ga•ril´•a's sleeping dead while the car moves motor images faintest for the audile base runner who happens to be nearby close utterly separated running in the emerald dark not augite some other infinite yet or as the man aulophyte existing seemingly without basis other than the deb's thought seeing him in a meadow having bathed he's butt-naked buff bending (to trim? what he'd called) "the eagle's feet" later somehow eagle the calcarate spur flies *in the place of* him. While *not* auger-eyed the base runner's the audile auscultates the vision enabling him to seize the entire sight-occurrence dependent-origination of the gelechild appearing either interrupted-zooming or still-freezing-emerald what are motor images? Any moving? Unknowing, the deb is Sleeping Beauty un-programmed or programmed too? He can examine all at once so aurochs black extinct move in the Aurora the gelechild visible by moving with these ox aurochs also at dawn? A banner cloud strays plume-shaped downwind from an isolated mountain peak. *Are* at dawn all of them jump-started different from omission in or ignited + in dark that which is moving (the gelechild's as *jumped-vaulted-over within space* possibly any are)? Is the base runner the auk diving birds audile (that is) in the existence of compassion, come + passion as audile seizing the entire sight-occurrence + while it moves its entire comprehension seized smelts the opposite of rigidity (which is) *can't exist*, Alice. As (at the instant) in regard to her declaring, compassion can't won't exist. Ever. That's *how* it does, its interior traveling.

# Coherer

L's statement of the idea of someone else's experience, or work of art they've made, is taken (L's idea) to be what created the work or memory of the other's experience; her summary supposedly *its clear* self, actually alien: as if L is the originator and the maker of its *real* self though its stream of occurrence unknown (occurrence itself is somehow obfuscation to them) is only later viewed as (or is to *be*) idea of it. A flesh-butterfly-several-occurrences (events melded) is not idea, not produced by idea, nor produced by L. Later, as person-flesh-butterflies halving series, there is a new idea—yet not L's, separate. Whether aural experience or written, hybrid someone-else's-flesh-butterflies-war say is as grappled senses if in language at all. As language it has to be other senses always. Only instigation the coherer isn't dictation [the radio detector operated by the base runner]. The handlers of L seeing the maker of the action or work a mere artisan (of/and for others), the brain of it supposedly in L hierarchically is separated the dihedrons float. Occurrence believed to be derived from someone's later ideation of it (that supposedly makes it, the separated synopsis is the disappeared occurrence later or *real*-ly) is attributed, that person's celebrated thrives the gazelle-dihedrals come into being stemming though they come in forward. They depart in the hoarse fretting of the ropes on the hog at the sea's edge the small white wolfdog appears hesitant runs sideways 4 originating in snow freezing sleet-plain the wolfdog fearing masses of water delighted now at the edge, where she gives one bark to welcome the surfboarder boy coming in on the flattened foam endlessly generated the boy arises from his surfboard looking admiringly or wistful awed glow of half-smile at greeting him the little dog eagle overhead who've led the laughing base runner in the emerald zone suddenly to deorbit popping blown onto the sand. They are from the glass tube of the coherer. L's split invisible to herself, it could be that for L (for her, idea being higher, being is base) it is inconceivable that mere occurrence is in relation to idea *ever*, so L perceives an idea that emerges in the unfolding of occurrence—as her own. If she can't ever see it (occurrence) she does not perceive it as her flesh. Ocker (redundant) is in having a bun on wandering in the forest when the scavenging little girls some toothless still recognizing the kidnapper of children it's only been moments 4 he makes no distinction much less regret drop their net from a tree to hogtie the peewit lier les quatre pattes recognized *in terms of* an earlier experience netted breathing spiritus asper yet creates a wave crest a bumboat coming to them over the waves of sea forms from the waiting freighter to pick the girls up in order (to capture them) who're running from the dogfaces (sighted on the beach, the girls have flown, run) and in an other freighter an other time stevedores loading the grain that's falling on them as rain in echopraxia repetition of shadows' actions loading standing in the ship's hole the grain rains on them each could only be interpreted at their end but being interconnected no action has an ending its supposed idea (that is of an occurrence before or outside) is socially conveyed as the single original source a product, as its idea, that to the orphan girls is an incomprehensible rule of body-mind split gazelle-dihedrals have no birth. Some of the girls confused by the split become enraged though others overflow it as dysaphic reefs only. even as such. having no tactile no hearing seeing senses—*as* this even, they override. no here base runner senseless now known brought to the drift world by the Distaffer 4 sensually held him/having been held by him in black ocean but he himself sees between the lids outside-eyelids (outside's eyelids) as equally death and being alive in events he's held fluttering bleeding from the atmosphere entry moving through the occluded waking in the night I was lying with the sense of utterly happy to be alive for no reason the occluded is there they see the roaming flayed open gazelle-dihedrals as large as prehistoric terror birds that ran eating the small horses it's raining yet his landing coming through onto the rainless sand-beach in surf here has popped through the emerald membrane 4 the base runner has also the coherer radio detector with a glass tube by means of which they later transmit detecting from it the opposite of his motion dictation stealing from the glass tube empty social half-life beginning from the illusion of "imaginative flight leading to mundane life" *as if that were good!* the one person hierarchical finalizes *is* the official view, is *described* as limitation (as if good), anything other incomprehensible as some invisible self bad-ridden at once. Ground. Grind basis. As it happens, not invigilating. Madariaga, it's a lost action transplants ferrying for the leukemic children their transplants long practiced become impossible because having to be on an officially approved instrument, the instrument they use/have used for years suddenly not approved, they'll die. Dogface the infantrymen run in the surf. Toward them. To the girls they are dogfaces. The base runner elucidating that is his other face creates transplants of leukemic children at once the coherer to which is attached the glass tube the emerald membrane inspan of the draught animals to a vehicle in a field becoming green below glow in after-dawn a kind of core dump dropping all memories not a doge rather the brilliant the base runner all the time 4 instants having no reason other than love, 4 the gelechild unknown enters his heart's lake there can't be duplicated nor is there any desire on their part to repeat his entire heart's lake trafficked in the coherer's glass tube alone. they are.

# Limen

Amor Asteroid transfixing her gaze not auger-eyed anyway the soft eyes on either side muzzle panning the horizon having to turn for her powder monkey boy jockey, having been taken from him, who'd been removed from the track, she'd begun cribbing wind-sucking in deliration, they figured, so another jockey aulophyte takes her into the deliquescing hills become dawn before them before other hills and rearing on one of the hills she trots transformed—to be the race horse Amor Asteroid—from the small dazzlingly white flying wolf-dog the air cribriform she also appears sieve-like first as the trotting wolfdog shimmering for an instant then returns to this aulophyte (the substituting jockey) the piebald contumacious phosphorescent as shooting the hills cribriform 4 descending a hill one becomes katabatic wind the shooting horse transforms a head. Sky is brought together in one's night-dream while awake seeing that dream in the next day, concentrating (on dreaming to have the night pushed into day) which one can't do now or has dropped. Any addition a hyphenate up goes a clay pigeon shot breaking apart above in the dusky-dawn air one hole in it, the family ocker analphabetic sensory blinders on his peepers though screwing around the man taken advantage of clay pigeon also is in shooting practice everything transformed by its being at once the hispid running ocker transferring his loyalties to anything arising. Near-by. The base runner the Distaffer in the night alone when it is alone the ootheca spews ootid scents in spring day and night sky that's the limen there. Or the limen is there anyway. Oar through the limen the competitive ocker hispidulous garde-filled at entry even decides to own and mount Amor Asteroid having never ridden. He hasn't yet. Coinciding with the goal as the memory of getting to Lo-Munthang (that hasn't occurred) its entry (there) is by horse or by plane the airfare too expensive for them.

# Dysaphic

Emiction of the huge stamping Clydesdales it flying back in the blue or black decrement yet they flow forward stride a woman her blonde hair tied in a thick horse tail her sturdy thighs planted striding evenly resembles coming toward one on the sidewalk passing reassembles the forward-moving line of the blonde-maned Clydesdales the little girls on the sidewalk guide the stalks ties to balloons that glide up the sidewalk one day thick rippling Clydesdales having no bobbery or emendation the emitter may be the little girl sucking a cachou the city turned estancia surveyed by someone else, the tall deb her eye scanning momently before she turns with the thought in her eye seeing the Clydesdales still for an instant as in trompe l'oeil I could be in cladogenesis achieved in sight while the emoticon of the red wrathful petals afar opening and closing sieve of dysaphia caducous close to caduceus embryotoxic the cattle emit the young hopeful untied no emolument and with purity that the Clydesdales also will have. Do.

# Limen

The corner of one eye reflects to the brain a little girl on the sidewalk shooting by the side of a white and black-spotted dog, the seer repeating thoughts orally inside is the seer's echolalia of the little girl's actions rather than the little girl's sight, the girl and the black and white-spotted dog run together on the sidewalk in echograph of outside as that ocean depth (the outside) where the little girl fetal worm curls in sonic waves a woman riding a black and white the spotted pinto or paint rearing wheeling on it pats its side—the seer's echopraxia is to repeat these actions, of the little girl and her as the woman riding the white-black-spotted pinto as seer of the rider 2 (to) repeat the actions riding (seeing herself). Riding and didn't know riding. At first echolalia, spoken. The transfection is echopraxia as uncontrollable repeating of actions as people are speaking or silent seeing that action a space transforms? Such as the deb being sustentacular to the base runner in the emerald dark.

Therefore single events, that don't exist anyway, are paradise—*are* at all (by such) and are paradise. Entry. And being in a single event any.

The eye of passerby records the little girl running beside the black-white-spotted dog or the little girl from a different point of view (hers and one's) seeing and/or speaking/running—but being beside the dog is no mere record, being/action. So action isn't only fundamental to being. It's outside individuals while at once them. To be an event outside simultaneous, no space exists between an individual's action and that as event with others—'then' is both. Their actions the event echopraxia each repeating a single motion randomly infinitely and as it has no connection of its parts or to other motions, *where* it doesn't, it wears through to a place of an invisible motion before its forming.

## Violet violently unforming

The butterfly blood-reef red Chrysanthemum is always lies lying so there is no self of the forming young one who needs that or, 4 without it, is lost in violence. Or butterfly blood-reef of lies so there occurrence as process of/in is no duration or single event with one in it. None.

By not having connection, and wearing through to a place of an invisible action from appearing a single link in the interdependence, an unknown action transpires—the spotted dog the spotted dog looks at itself?

The paradise, among many any possible, is that. Seeing at all—and in single movements (that can't exist anyway, in interdependence) so apprehended in series or sequences only the spotted dog looks 'then.' The butterfly blood-reef is 'then' dazzling illumined. Which is at times.

The attacks in Mumbai by a single group, on a restaurant, a cultural center, and a hotel, many killed, included the terrorists, all except one—who must afterwards have been tortured—one of the attackers a boy lying asleep on the engine of a car in the street having died when before at the moment the car moving its engine starting, having started and died as the driver *wishes* to escape to elude the events motionless in mind-lit-aura (to repeat in cacography as squiggly lines started in a notebook), the boy sleeping in death-response has set in motion or the engine does gore as strainer echopraxia the emerald dark dilating—to retrieve him? Oar to have him living? as imitating the motion of his life by repeating each motion?

# Augend

The Distaffer however wracked with memory as whole gliding iceberg beneath the surface from which single on the surface cracking appear flinching butterfly involuntary memories these consecutively torment her sometimes at once this trait-occurrence existing (+ is her) apart from the audile the base runner calm only running auscultates examines draws visually-motor the gelechild (not, if not seen) or all the bur-like fiery with it and the visual and motor images the entire emerald dark or independent the gelechild equally tormented? Or *she* torments? tore the dihedrons and gazelle-dihedrals visual and motor images there begin (without him and *with* him, the base runner) to singe in *ward* physically inwardly as flesh of burning petals evaporate the dihedrons feel depths of excruciating physical pain unknown to the butterfly or petals. There tore the image of them the gazelle-dihedrals also. They need him *to be*. In order for them to *be* (as sequence also). The audile base runner simply hears them while he's running moves open they appear to vanish? Without burning backward or forward move inward to vanish. In front of him the rose and green planes moving onto the same time plane everywhere. Whole they're not seen calm gentle gazelle-dihedrals zoom are gone

# Flesh space

Is like a plug that has been released [or has] released all in ward or out ward/the floor ripped out consequence or mobile that everything has poured out attached to kites in which the eagle is walking in the midst of the annatto orange-red fields of grass that's the present blowing the blown almost horizontal oar (same as 'or' silent) quiescent? A grave mark is there. There there's also the annatto orange-red grass that stretches in invisible wind.

## The float

Muscular nude except wearing a mask also butterfly striped wings that stood straight above his head yet appearing to her having survived that had not died, he hadn't died, her relief at this as reminiscent of a figure emerging in red non-land appears to be whorl out of it seeming red or a figure walking in black endless sparkling solid not either sky-wall or land the emerging figure appears to be is part of its surroundings/ from it illumined outline in black surroundings filled his is flesh having recovered from throat cancer. A man wears a lion's head. As sequence, in sequence, a single event is paradise. The head has become him near-by. There was no past. People near them fight bicker as if this/of the people's actions has already happened is on-going in the days around them/these two by them selves an owl drifting by zooms the field then even there being no single event is—motor movement there, paradise.

*(bottom)*

## Food

The base runner is starved having used up his reserves. They sit the three (the Distaffer and deb also) together eating in a restaurant

## The eye

They'd gone out to supper in the early closing of the shops takes her seeing a candy-striper canon cancrizans no dystrophy at all then the cruiserweight the candyman's response dysuria a piss-take rather but the cruiserweight resisting turns him away a candyman comes parascending parasailing in a clearing of the emerald dark appears whole rippling in place and unharmed cruiserweight (having) flies in bursts into flame briefly [there is in day also] a turquoise owl because (eye) thought of it.

## Author's note close to the end, before Cromorne

*The Dihedrons Gazelle-Dihedrals Zoom* was written by
words being chosen at random from the dictionary in a process of alexia,
not as mental disorder but word-blindness—to make an unknown
future—yet making as it happens sensual exquisite corpses
led to the discovery that there *isn't* any future, isn't even any present.
Such an exquisite corpse, read, is in an instant yet not even in 'a present.'
Outside's events unite gluing to each other a single object.
That which had already existed is by chance.
The exquisite corpses are physical as if one such is flesh-butterfly-other-
(real-time events such as the attack on Mumbai), each such event-cluster
internally hybrid rather than being separate presentation as idea.
That is,
the writing is not the idea of the whole framework of occurrences after
without its existence ever being. In the accumulating stream of events,
hybrids repeating parts of an event in different combinations,
the parts rearranged by imagination begin to *pierce* each other surpassing
single outlines and boundaries, the sense of infinite combinations are actions
bliss. *That which had already existed is by chance*: not only includes events in
real-time but visual scenes existing *before* the writing—Jess's collages
that show parts of the reality though different scenes of it infinitely unfolding
as randomly discovered composite actions. Masami Teraoka's painting of an
octopus sucking a woman's front was a memory occurring simultaneous
with the instant of writing it: is seeing our memories making the present.
The characters have *this* sensual memory though they are without memory
unknown sensual object as it comes up found by *its* language, its being at once

language and physical object generates in continuous stream of attachments—
in which the "base runner" (the words chosen at random
from *Random House Webster's Unabridged Dictionary*),
[he's] one of the people generated by the sensory-word-passages,
perceives through a coherer radio detector with a glass tube.
Robber barons rewriting history—that doesn't exist anyway—
the greed of wanting to dissolve others no one existing except them,
everything, beings, including one's being are (have become) lies
Cheney's eyes, in his head also, one of his eyes floats in the palm of
the viewer—the lies are part of the split between one's physical being
and one's seeing (mental and physical sights)
people on every level suffering from this as isolation.
The isolation: We're taught to think as hierarchy. Idea-as-information
is domination supposedly, seizure, by mundane life a version of idea
derived from military models of targeting; a sensory-language-physical-
object would be incomprehensible (*is* now) unless translated to be
description of/as its purpose. Translate a whole flesh-butterfly-other-
hybrid outside of its being, outside its language *here*—Lisa—translate it
to be its *idea* of its action—as if the *other* language, of it outside it,
is its structure or theory, its *real* self, while the occurrence-hybrid-itself
*may be* an idea but as only its whole framework of occurrences later.
Where we cannot see the use or relation of imagination to idea/*occurrence*,
the gazelle-dihedrals are open organs all visible
in frames human-like that zoom forward as plains of sight action
Roaming, they may be suffering or there's terror everything opened
by here being sensorial flattening blissful also in common people's
seizure to summarize any thing extrapolating the sensual object without being
"*now*" is mere illusion of its encapsulation ahead future—
that doesn't exist anyway—without pretext

# Cromorne

The events of the section "Cromorne" (a Renaissance musical reed instrument, horn, having a cylindrical tube bent or crooked at the end) are happening/are to be read as happening at the same time as events in the main body of *The Dihedrons Gazelle-Dihedrals Zoom*. Throughout simultaneous with the latter's extended stream, the events of "Cromorne" form simultaneous pairs with some, now new, events of the main text.

# Cromorne, Eyelids the bud

Unknown whether the Mrs. goes along with this rhamnose (they call him) selling the little girls at the back door rewarranted or rewashed they disappear into the current market of orphaned later slaves from which cycle they had been fleeing lying on the bed-sheets the bulb breathing ("Give them to us" had cried Madame Secretary, opening—the *only* orphanage? though each year there are millions abandoned) the one's bud senses clearly all the events as does its flaring blossom of one any opened in this excruciating physical dense pain the blossom breathing fully is it the bud its alternate decreases collecting that flood of excruciating pervading deadening pain damps it down the bud black or pink being it only though within its curled soft small flesh that cannot contain the pain the spine run through it broken once of someone else's reverberating perceives it is not the object or origin of the clear perception that disseminated no diluent it cannot have halve be dolus the flaring pink blossom of/in utter pain takes in animating all of the outer events (either coal dense bud does or flared open blossom in these perceived) others far from its flare the blossom's edges that are not generated from itself but from out there that generating pools of the girls bathing in the attack on Mumbai in the natural crevasse falls thundering water on the bobbing lilies the terrorist ga•ril´•a boy in Mumbai lies in gore on the car's engine asleep the float bowl of the carburetor flooded those halving animation or those still that are between animation and day senses flares/blossom rose or other animates it/day one moon of Saturn swims beside it. By the bed-table there is a book called *Eyelids of Dawn* [about] crocodiles pictured lying on banks alter the dawn itself. The night monkey, the huge owllike eyes closed in sleep, lay on the bed-sheet alongside a row of little girls holding rifles asleep eyelids move in dreams the floating rib frozen not of the rhebok grazing on the lawn outside that floats under one of the moons of Saturn only dichromic vision in looking at it the Mrs. who keeps a nighthawk relentless ruthless goatsucker while housing thousands of the little girls in her dovecote may not know serving them milk that her husband skulks a rhinorrhea spout pouring the girls are on floats holding the reins of horses that are carried on the floats rhathymia theirs reweaving their events or weaves the events current light-heartedness rheo-flow furling the open full pink blossom extended it blows.

# The black rhebok

Nicostratus with his illegitimate half-brother had expelled Helen from Sparta. Her own son expelled her. After his father's, Menelaus's death. After Paris. After Troy. I didn't know that. She's lying in the bed next to theirs, the thousands of little girls passing through housed in the Mrs.'s dovecote, a row of them the girls in bed with rifles there. In the morning Helen animated wane sad or slouching carefree inclinable looks in the mirror as surrounded by the little girls combing their hair, giglets tying their boots in groups to Helen jackanapes (archaic Helen's giglet 2) a jack-a-dandy slick scansorial as lover, met in a café the Jabberwocky of the children some with scarlatina drowns him in the krummholz stunted forest the kouprey blackish-brown body with white markings on the back and feet wild Kore Kôr´ Core Korah in rebellion leads the girls away when at the instant of their being they're lighthearted scanning line-single horizontal trace made by the electron beam in one traversal of the fluorescent screen. Watch one of the orphans ride. Watch rides Amor Asteroid a race horse having gotten lost plows with the girl riding bareback the canyons of oil petroleum fields bombed having set loose in predation the oil spurting islets flood the land mired the black rheboks stand the children swim in it.

# The Ceratosaurs

While rhamnose, called by them, grows rich. A floating rib breathing in the rhinorrhea flow mischanter delivers the doped girls to them. Imitation doublet gem from a single piece of glass immeasurable when Watch had first looked down into the glass percolator having named herself Demi-hunter considered too intellectual renamed by the others Watch had seen horses moving a merry-go-round in the glass percolator akin to the night monkey's eyes while looking down swift ferocious ceratosaurs killing maiming the country continued enslaving more child-soldiers who amputating murdering are by their own murderous acts a caste of children bound to the military can't ever return home desmoid a small boy who is a fibrous sheet ligamentous red buff carries a machete hacking saphenous vein within any passing citizen in his range these pour the saphenous veins near a child-soldier riding a capybara whose webbed feet ascend the hygric slopes from which Gigantes limbs the trees cut weaving the wind in which a giereagle sits on one limb probably Egyptian.

# The Ceratosaurs

Ceriferous jack-a-dandy appearing dead from his wax gland spruced stands of a stadium flaring sides in the bright sunlight everywhere the waxed men run. In it. The stadium filled with cheers. Arising herd floats on the air. Having kidnapped them made child-soldiers of them who killing maiming amputating carry AK-47s the multitude of children-soldiers forever lost the men leading this civil war havoc on the 2 sides forced to the peace table by the women dally fritter all hotel expenses paid until the women lock them in the negotiating hall surround them groups of women in a sit-in stop the doors the women unarmed brave imitable each wear the T-shirt on which is written PEACE. Where formerly the women had sat for peace by the sides of the road sometimes in pouring rain the cars filled with armed men pass who are the killers ceratoid president or rebel leader either on the road with no cerecloth raincoats the rain covered the women both men swift carnivorous 20-foot length ceratosaurs with livid scars while the child-soldiers cut off the appendages of citizens their own appendages circus tactile organs which many child-soldiers lose. Child-soldiers too lose legs. Or oar empty invisible arms. Cerynean stag. Seen in the stadium amidst the men. Disappears. Seen on the road stands in the rain. By everyone. Regardless of AK-47s. Held on them or holding them on others.

## Black dew

Is it rhebok rheboks the jack-a-dandy groupie silly-putty adapted scansorial lover climbing on Helen's flesh adapted to social climbing butts the buttes are crumbling facades red in the horizontal trace lit fluorescent screen of the universe 2 (to) profit as predation of all the creatures in it covered in oil deluging mire spouting the birds the 2 walk beneath Saturn but Venus cool in the night bright sails while in day dark with the petroleum of the fields let loose Venus is still? Cold night. A breeze lights on them in future. Watch who walks in petroleum fields and emerges black as covered with dew. 4 as a child one hasn't emotion or it is as crystals clinging crumbling at touch remembered as a flesh object 4 there is no death. Later emotion is separated defined to saponify. for some reason. Or time is something else fuse giglet archaic lascivious as Helen sapid. All the time some people wasting it one literalizes time by pretending to be in prison frittering waste of days intentionally while others really *are*. Dual, their choice of pretending, is to show time being empty and absurd but as tactile the black dew covering one the little girl orphans each black beach dew jewel bead having been pressed squeezed the black or pink bud one breathes though the dense excruciating physical disorienting—the fact of this pain phenomenally occurring, as also a man *actually* by choice sitting for a year in a room furnished as a prison time photographed is a basis—that one contained as the bud damped from one's full flailing blossom open wild with it as soft small flesh is curled in the crazed empty dense then light blossom's extension as senses not emotion not itself alone but as outside brought to a head open with petals flair. But or so 4 a child there is no death [and] going on always—ever, especially when in the midst of it around all the children not just from scarlatina scarlet fever or the beaver fever from both ends the livid scarlet scarification of emaciated beggars dying starving everywhere on the street corners too.

# For now

For now, the night monkey coming through the window, the pet of the Pecksniffian Mrs. however eyes owllike night monkey drools flops and droops miming the effect of the milk the unctuous Mrs. serves thousands of little girls she calls her puckish hatchlings bedded in the dovecote but only a few observe the warning the tiny night monkey gives dew-covered in his antics the others enter sleep dinoflagellates Noctiluca exuding light the bedded group going out into night causing luminous appearance of that hydrozic sea their sleep. In dawn the dewdrops reflecting the sun's beams will stud the fields with billions of rainbows from each dewdrop blue violet yellow rose flows of infinity. A dogsbody labors with a dustbin outside their midget rooms in the dovecote where outside the gigawatt that is many X (times) gigawatt Jupiter swims in the rhinosporidium while lacing in the bead lightning Watch who hasn't drunk the milk listening to the night monkey taking it the tiny douroucouli in her arms Watch, Des Moines they're named after the cities their intended destination to which they will be sent later as slaves—already would be except they've run away—will again Watch who isn't transported who will run away elude

run through the fields whose valves open and flood after them, traps set that open to flood them ascend to night

# Seam

Zebras' stripes make them invisible when they stand or run hardly flicker motive beings—You dope!—votive beings though the child-soldiers originate from the men ceratosaurs forcing them to rampage to kill to live, rather than to live to die, not quite imagining this the children, bound by their committing these acts half guilt fear of apocatastasis and no fear (both at one) oiled by cocainism, some, 4 being young dove-tailed as easily put a butt shaft in a man or woman with love-handles catenulated chain of command none 4 aposematic colored as zebras' stripes seams invisible when the boys stand or run motive being in the large groups of child-soldiers young carpetbaggers who're murderous becomes discretionary fashion to choose douze-pers to order the child-"campaigns" when gape-mouthed ceratosaurs-men are absent child-leaders divide booty ripped off from stray families or men or women individuals encountered called "lambs." The child-soldiers are lawless pre-knowledge where "the Kyprian" undiluted hot desire ranging among the birds raving loose doesn't need a machete to do it. More likely the douze-pers fight each other to the relief of the smaller ones they fight over a chair lifted from someone's house.

## A tawny saunter

A bobcat the length of a cougar a tawny rippling saunter emerges from the Gigantes forest-motion of forest and the cat's slink casting the head that riding on its low-set flanks-frame then on its motionless stretched frame upright basks in the dew-covered yellow light dazzling field before it. There is no 'in,' nothing within. Of course the rhinorrhea spewing horn the floating rib breathing in it had stabled the racehorse Amor Asteroid after the Mrs. coaxed the little girl to come down. The orphan dismounting having ridden for days lost come from an Aegean stables where eluding the first deportation had first named herself ________ [missing] altering the name Lima numbered 213 later Watch runs away with the powder monkey boy bug bear who sees her in a window and comes to the sill he's riding Amor Asteroid introduces her sleeping nights together in trees with the stars in day to the horses as groom in the stables of the fat-cats, there are solely men who're also slavers directing the deportations of orphaned girls slaves a sea in days of heaven the indigo blue sky on the gold ground the 2 powder monkey and girl ride bareback the racehorse Amor Asteroid guides. How did the horse lose the girl? Now. (A picture shone.) Tripping, one foot in a gopher hole? No. Dazzled by seeing something? No or yes. Troupe of child-soldiers banging pots and pans to distract the child and horse so they fall . . . . . . ?

# More listen

Listens to the peanut gallery the night monkey climbing all over it threaded as vascular polyps in the nasal passage of rhamnose rhinosporidium a sea of the horn spews. A sign pinned to her chest "Won't speak." Watch whose name officially is Lima 213. Goes with Des Moines and the Bronx other orphan girls into the cover of the Gigantes trees limbs in the hygric night the canvas oriented movements hydrotactics of the coursing Jupiter Portuguese man-of-war now in air-streams and in or by parachronism the little girls in the cover of the Gigantes trees catch a glimpse viewed in the parting limbs of child-soldiers carrying AK-47s emigrating flight rather transporting lines of them behind them in the sky hydroskiis lighting night like fireflies in which the planes' parachute brakes open horizontally. Skidding to a stop on night itself. Planes taxi there. Seeing the details of faces lighting a dog's breakfast, murmurs the smallest child, Los Altos viewing the hodgepodge ("dog's breakfast," murmurs Los Altos again) in the midst of which the menial boy-drudge the dogsbody is trapped and baited pavid a boychild who in school did seatwork nicely but had been consigned to drudgery here is baited by the child-soldiers they see one riding the Cerynean stag a boy a conchy (who's a child-soldier though). Pterodactyl the pterosaurs having a very long 4th finger each without motors yet sag rising sawing as guttering violins swim the sky the mine-dusters had cleared for them, the military. Had cleared of all life except them, selves. Flit heavily is 2 times. Moving is more. So they move.

# For listening

For listening to dourouCouli the tiny night monkey carried at the tiny girl's ear wade by the open valves of night opening even further to expose the stadium filled with the hungry thirsting airlifted by low-slung choppers from the flood that swimming with corpses—Watch suddenly is swimming with night monkey curled on her neck riding in unknown parachronism imbricating the corpses floating into whose sunken submerged faces she'd once looked or will with powder monkey boy accompanying to see herself in the dead—is it future?—without washing to sea the layered flood of biofilms, on the banks when they're finally delivered by the waves Amanita muscaria the red mushrooms spotted-with-yellow grow while around them from the armies of little orphan girls running some hungry having eaten the poisonous Amanita muscaria some naked loosened their clothes without pudeur seated gymnosophists a stand-alone upright still eating; the others lie sleeping hallucinating dead that beam back information. A goiter on an old woman. A ball falling. A hoyden who in this apiology the flip-flop finds herself alongside mischanter yet untouched by the nighthawk of the Mrs. who peccant or innocent unknown keeping an eye on the hoyden nighthawk will look into the owllike eyes of night monkey, also the belonging of the Mrs., the Mrs. who looks up at night sees the white bars on the inner wings and the forked tail flowing of this rare Antillean it will call in the dark sky pity-pit-pit the open halves of actions at last meaningless!

## Hoyden yet who not meeting mischanter... as hoyden {substitute} 'when' *meeting* mischanter

Watch who *is* taken for a hoyden by the Mrs. the benefactress of the girls, not miscited, another smaller girl in terror running away toils up a hill on the other side of which the guns are heard firing. Reaching the top of the hill she would be killed except a hoyden (not Watch) bravely runs after the small fleeing child and swift as the Mrs.'s Antillean nighthawk seizing that smallest child at the crest crescent moon on it returns with her. (Who'd saved her) The Tomboy Dallas a child herself, the Mrs. *is* glad but a sort of secret horror held reserved in her toward that hoyden the same who 'then' 'when' *meeting* mischanter *is* untouched by the floating nighthawk cruising later time a reservoir of such horror in the Mrs. *is* not for the Antillean nighthawk, the cup enormous basin of the blossom vast outside the perimeters that which *is* the extraordinary (the physical, in one an instance when it *is* pain) dropping out/but the extraordinary 'drops out' to the outside on the flared edges of the blossom that the dense released this time boundless physical pain overwhelming everywhere as the one (image *is* meaningless) who *is* small soft flesh one's in the center (not image while it's there) hoyden or other character traits or life are unrelated to the enormous blossom empty wild excruciating pain nor *is* the flesh or the bone that frame of the small body producing this vast fully open blossom or not producing its alternate now and then occurring, that *is* its own blossom's *later* bud contracting yet not containing that intense pain the pink bud or it's purple-black damping the excruciating to be later or at some other time (where there *is* no time, now) the utterly open flaring blossom there (already), concentrated. Asked what is the pain like, it is like the dazzling blue indigo baby Shiva floating on an emerald green leaf in the sea of the universe outside meaninglessly lovely. Bob thinks a particular condition seen as producing or responsible for some one person's experiencing physical pain, he thinks one cause (or person with that cause) *is* of a greater magnitude as having even higher deference (social) comparatively than another. One having scoliosis an entire bar in her back he cites as if a shorter bar, or as if bars removed/ their absence, or a fracture—as if they did not measure as significantly as hers (with scoliosis hers *is* the entire bar) in such comparison—*is* for him/overseeing *as*/description that's itself the act of cultural-mind-body-split schizoid while (whereas) physical pain at its most excruciating level is boundless has no cause. in the sense of that (cause) being irrelevant. At that level *is* (boundless). 'then.' To those within—scofflaw, refers to the word "within"—who are that level itself/are that pain {there is no 'within' no 'without'}, there are no comparisons—yet experience now having no value and particularly pain devalued as we're puritans, there *is* no speaking/no speaking in people experiencing (*is* said by outsiders) the most excruciating possible being outside bounds *is* unrelated to cause, to outside or to speaking. has no cause. Nor *is* there any depersonalizing ever, Elaine, the huge open blossom *is* unrelated to personalizing or depersonalizing being one 4 the mind strangely there may be alert in or *by* the wildly distracted being. Being distracted. Beside it. Self. Utterly alert. Therefore action—reaching the crest of the hill/unrelated but *is* action/ opened running to it Dallas to seize the child who'd running toward the firing guns had fled in terror from the Mrs. [the civilians (meaning also the little girl here fleeing the Mrs.) eluding round-up running actually *toward* the war, the battlefield no image *Wade-Giles* later can be (*is*—would be already) 'when'] but Bob explains that Kathy does not have pain. One could not "identify" with hers, after a game not as with her "self" there *is* no one there for only matter material hers he says in ***being only social*** (he describes) no suffering of self can occur. Empty. He speaks in the place of/ that experiencing. As if *is* it, without it being there. *Is* it not being there. Therefore he makes it occur. In women, girls, he makes the open blossoms go to *their* buds. They're beside each other everywhere. There their physical pain if a cliché everything is a cliché. "Self"-defined social *is* suffering. That's what "self" *is*. As his. Thus 2.

## The Steersman

A girl, before the white distaffer had come into being as that (before she is that—someone separated, as her being—and separated by others), asked accepted danced in front of the silent rage-filled Afrikaners on the ship's deck dance-floor empty except for them the thirteen-year-old dancing with the black young college student whose shaking wracked frame trembling sweat-bathed hardly able to move dancing knows living in the eternal apartheid reinstituted future whereas the partner girl pre-slave almost-child sees the conditions and is untainted and uncontained by them (conditions or people) as without inkling of their passion. The next day thrown against the wall by the Afrikaners pinning pummeling her in the ship's hall. Soon after, disembarking she's elsewhere in a boat on a stream, the steersman black, and a fat hoggish huge enraged Afrikaner brimming tore into her with the hoggish hatred verbal assaults accosting her though she's seated in the boat doing nothing the man pushes his obscene bulk as it were beating them rants on the inferiority base nature the low less than animals who are black the steersman's face averted he's still his body motionless screen while he's working steering beside them in the boat its motor leading them gliding—then she learned rage. And her own being—hidden by her raising a screen as the steersman does before the hate-filled abhorrent Boers' abuse of her and the steersman. Rage isn't in her but is born then. Comprehending that passion she notes nothing. It *is* apart from her and towards him who is violating them. As if she had thought. "She could leap on him." Yet she's open and unformed ahead. Then but it is still future she flooded behind the screen.

## Her fastness

Waking with the embryo by her in its chorion, so its being, still, enveloped wrapped in its membrane concealed could be a reptile, bird, or mammal; while flustered, she knows it is not hers—the Distaffer has a singular, sharp yet otiose memory of an Aunt Jane rigid decorous young regal moonrat crippling others by her corrosively flippant certainty dismissive of them to them alongside her view of herself recruited by one of the leaders of a group like rotary as her being very small shown in their moonrise. Whatever fastness the Distaffer has, the finding out of her being, that is always *before* either ahead or prior and at once, in which the Distaffer in separation performs whatever fare-thee-well in whatever moonwalk her way resembling the weightless movement of walking on the moon, the Aunt Jane looks only to the monstrance of the leader exposed briefly by him for her veneration. Not lover of the leader, the Aunt Jane who is knowingly humbly too low for that, she's the graceful [grateful] honored runt receiving only haughty meager approval from him. In the Aunt Jane's utter certainty that the Distaffer is neither like a leader nor accepted by his rotary, the Aunt Jane elegant small chorister to it has disdain and pride in her neat though hollow prudery of only imitating his directives. Until they're old. Intending to demonstrate the Distaffer's useless separateness as not within the frame of the endeavor, the Aunt Jane, determined, pursing her lips had declared her own role of "responsibility" to this frame. Responsibility to subjugation of the being that erased only directed repetition of other's invisible limb is to be static? had wondered the Distaffer saying nothing. Why does the Distaffer mind, given her fastness utter pleasure in her moonwalk the weightless unknown movement? It is not because there is some desire still for communion montane with them, given up. In this particular unrelated memory, she recognizes she had wished to change the Aunt Jane fundamentally; she had tried to change that one leader fundamentally by everything being, in her mind, moot point subject to debate or dispute ocean of reason. "Example of unknowing as dor (nonsense or folly, certainly Catch-22)." a friend had commented, though ocean of reason really exists outside. Though her sole memories now cause the actions in the outside as stream. Tried to change it without her doing, as *causing*, that action of the outside.

## "the like"

Therefore the present doesn't exist. Its *not* existing is felt and future slavery as the basis of its seaming only seeming system all the girls abandoned as infants by parents who in poverty or chance mischanter hadn't rigged the births to be male otherwise aborted or killed at birth, such female deaths occurring yearly in the millions the population soon weighted with pampered boys yet kidnapped these are sometimes sold to boy-less couples to later wait on them, when aged wait on the-purchasing-parents. Or kidnapped boys are forced to become child-soldiers once committed bound to their own murderous acts outside 'society'/the jewel civilization they're lost forever. ?? *We don't know that.*

Far from seeking entry to civilization therefore the girls are __________

Not only to be outside the jewel/civilization ____________ that lost forever there isn't death in it either (the children imagine)—the goal is flight for some or 4 (for) others scordatura senses are deathless any senses sight tactile hearing the blossom empty wild opening to make the bud the edges rushing of the florid displayed outside of one's blossom of/on one person. —supposedly, which hadn't a present ever? So there isn't death either? or being in it. But they're all outside it, the parents etc. Bursting elated red-dark leaves the red-orange leafy trees throughout one (that's senses) elated outside everywhere that's one as spine is in it/is it open utterly awake!—the endless life the cool cold day illumined in the red-dark leaves orange bursting elated vault fall.

Des Moines had thought—she thought: the sconce would be at least a small detached fort within whose halls blank {her sensibility blank here except} laughing many orphan girls winding the spiral there protected from the child-soldiers and their handlers any of the warring sides (Des Moines had never wept). When they come to it the sconce proves to be just a protective screen on a hard-wind-blown plain—no, Detroit and Dakota both at once saying sconce the fine each child pays in the Mrs.'s etiquette school for any breach when the scout calls back to them from within or rather behind—there are many lying on the grass—behind the sconce screen the skulls sconces the size of children's heads dot the knoll has no verb but in sconce inside and outside drop out that fold on itself making itself by virtue—of oars—the Cerynean stag stood at least motors blank the like motored by the scolex seen looking in the bud (the little girl named Dallas sees) and the blossom the same at once or entirely different at once which the children can't/don't feel there/empty physical excruciating pain not theirs yet the bud and blossom making each other in air sconce being by the tapeworm it's beside and by that "means" scolex imageless that would be people midst the anterior head-like segments having suckers hooks or "the like" eating in one child Dallas 318 wept "the like" itself scofflaw literal wormholes a scooter becomes blank as Pacific fish and low child's vehicle steered with handlebars descending the hilly air-stream a flow-chart of a hill they're swept on 2 in ripples of grass-wind the scordatura outside (inside? "Mind," Alice. as only action) all there blow. Are "dor," "mockery" and "beetle," at once. Why isn't it heard elsewhere the grazing herd?

## The boney labyrinth

They are small ponies that fall into the canyons. Douroucouli-listening entails the girl (Watch) whose personality while vivid is so far sucked into listening to the tiny night monkey that perched at her ear the night monkey carried on her shoulder hears the signals that come up from the dead ponies. **What?** Watch asks, bending closer. The signals float up from the canyon. Dictation in a manner of speaking a doozer. At Pechiney hospital, the head doctor, Alpha Hasimon Diallo, says: "Everyone needs to tighten their belts." Parachute-brakes on the tails of the planes open as the planes skid in blooms on the landing field. Next fields of opium poppies—it follows (if they land). No. Sports stadiums and swimming pools are signs of paternalism forms a single surface of their rewriting history silhouetted halves holograms of Las Vegas or Cleveland Lubboch the cities or girls as their names shimmer before them who, some dead from eating the Amanita muscaria red with yellow spots others high from drinking the urine of the now dead intoxicated on their urinated hallucinogen sit squatting in the air the little girls gymnosophists hover float readily hear the night monkey's dictation but from a distance. Everything is before them us everyone 'before' being.

The sort of Lana Turner sulking sultry intellectual sweater-girl innocent abused later-dowager, the quondam tight sweater highlighting by stiffened bra-pointed breasts implies having hidden the luscious firm soft ones, who manages grooming the orphan girls' rough curls harnessed them at the deportation center, they remember. The sort of Lana Turner having the standard of the quotidian as if paradise minimalized applies "*the quotidian*" to everyone, as if there were one such. She doesn't see that for some this has no existence. Poverty, maim, being a happy vagabond, all of which she deplores, may be their quotidian life to which they're accountable or will not have lived. It has never been experienced that hers is limited. Growing up in the most right-wing garden sheltered from any input yet she herself radical not even rebel having burst clean from it young she finds grief yet firmly scolds the "excitement" of others. The underlying accusation on her tongue overtly pressed against one is of one being "excited by war" or excited by pleasure is to be censured we're so puritan. She puts her tongue into the ear of the tiny future night monkey. She did already, the girls later realize. Whereas "the Kyprian" with many names is death and undestroyable raving loose wailing with fear hot desire rage all real excellent energy's pierced by her past, by event—or *not* pierced, Lana's experiencing was limited. As the senses mistrusted are born by doctrine, they emerge dysaphic she glottalizes them. Yet always born for the first time, there are no comparisons. Engine ravels, cylinders started by inserted glow plugs each singular, dormant. "**So?**" one wonders.

## Mana

Everything is before them us everyone 'before' being. So community of the orphans can't exist ahead? Look at it. Something has to. Mana fields come before them the fields that move in front of them. B unknown. The young woman later distaffer flier comes up in the night monkey's dictation as hologram of her earlier. Earlier when working in the salt mines at age fourteen an orphan 'before' the events free slave 'then' (afterwards is not heard by the night monkey) the enormous pinkening octopus that sucks her on her middle finds her a buoy—it's a hologram of the man base running—in the deep ocean sucks her to her surface. She's flier disporting and transporting shipments of the little girls until (future parachronism—derives from their cronies?) finally airlifting shipments of them instead to isles. There was only innocence in her is un-formed 'then' latter bloom the young as distaffer unacceptable to all if not outcaste on which borders of society unfolded there regarded acceptable photonic physical giddyheaded landing her plane giereagle Egyptian in the hygric luminous mass sea of dinoflagellates producing light bright Noctiluca amidst which the child-soldiers starved are gathering the Mana feeding on the dinoflagellates alongside competing with birds the Juncos and Black-capped Chickadees singing chicka-dee-dee-dee, murmurs orphaned Dallas 318 back-grounding come with the other stray orphans Des Moines Dakota all the Ds then New Orleans Watch having been swept in with them once was Lima 213 a few others at the edge of the Gigantes forest peering through its edge. Everything has no verbs no inner motion. By virtue. Of that. Being drawn shining out of them. It is outside. The distaffer. What is it motoring outside? with the pterosaurs? Opposite of their scordatura, working in a salt mine which affects all of the actions of people even en route to cities the trains let alone the child-soldiers who over-see the workers policed with machetes and AK-47s not the romantic-crucifixion mound of the gold mines shone. Nothing shines too 2. So he photographs the salt mines, work—arms of machines already sunk roll on treads in wet fields or arms of slaves who are over-seen being hacked off by children-soldiers immediately romantic 2 sickened bleeding within shone.

# Seam

Even the recent past is compressed squeezed to be the present. Later after the pool, Dallas hides looking out from the Gigantes forest limbs. Without apparent physical injury a douze-pers bedridden can't rise plucking at the blankets demonstrates carphology (the act of the hands outside plucking at the blankets) so the douser who sometimes breaks up the fights between the boys by clowning dogsbody the smallest boy they've relegated to drudge serving also this function of douser lies down and plucks at his blankets 2. Who'd been good at seatwork in school imitates this gibing floccillation motive being to stay votive in his bed out of the campaigns. No aposematic coloring, he's seven and wants a butty. They cut off one arm that's floating on the covers. At this, the girl Dallas, ten years old or so colored aposematic as they are zebras from their stripes invisible where they run or stand wears green crocodile bursting from the forest seam writhing twirling catenulating bumps-and-grinds defensive. Offensive aposematic bumps a crocodile's hide seam warts her. Harridan her first remembered spelling word spitefully shoving the little girl in the pool figures Dallas would be inside a crocodile's skin butt in pieces while the woman drones about being a god her audience bullies forcing her she claims to these hurtful visions that hurt *them*, outside the rainbow is only the relation of the sun rain and one position seeing the rainbow appearing to fall always ahead of one above in the black the nighthawk doesn't seize Dallas at the edge of the pool resting.

Gloveman fielder as if that were lutist played when not there lutenist at night. A lute desert when encountering people under the ball of the huge glowing bound moon on the street above while the base runner is at once on the playing field of the soundless emerald dark where he is trapped there are no glovemen there either the city street is empty dark when the base runner descends lustrating eagle in the same space where he'd been running in the emerald dark.

# Cromorne

The cricetid pneumotropic clinging at that place on the corpses flung on trash heaps the bud breathing in some of them still a crocodile extended onto the sidewalk the food line from a vector confectionery a crocodile file of children out for a walk breaks at the crosswalk where they wait wind-blown. Their prolegs abdominal ambulatory processes of caterpillars there on the wind-blown street the children our larvae on pillars walk beside the ambling yellow machine-caterpillars that go race on that street dig gutting it opening deep pools crocodiles come to the surfaced orphaned girl Dallas tadpole who's elsewhere but her pool-image superimposed on the street of children—while the little Dallas swims to and fro mid the crocodiles' snapping and twirling their twisting bellies to grasp her in their jaws the image of the "harridan" declaiming having come to one's brain the woman assuming godhead being from the desert small-town but ordinary claiming as a god harridan forgotten spelling word to know and to feel more than any other person, than all the peoples, in her branding our murderous actions in war and torture of others, yet even those tortured the families of those killed don't feel in comparison to her? Cromorne never wounding or is is always heard in the midst if there. Her logic her dead hurting her as preserved in a megalithic chamber tomb an action from which she dictates the future to reconstitute herself: *in future all the men will be dead*—she's being hurt *forced to have vision by her listeners*, for liking her *freely one is only a "bully,"* the women being only *of 'those'* men she'll be the only one living therefore pronouncing *no compassion or love will exist* only her loose cannonade emotion. That forms her cosmography not crystalline, wounds. everyone there at its bud the young son of a US socialite and Pakistani diplomat divorced, comes, the son with problems in Chicago who would as soon sell heroin did and prosecuted eluded jail would as soon sell the heroin as he would scout the raiding and bombing of Mumbai, which he did, killing 163 including the boy who was terrorist ga•ril´•a lying asleep on the car boy cosmonaut on its engine starts in gore. Selling heroin co-operating with the authorities son Headley'd eluded jail now turncoat again he turns in all those in the Mumbai plot the not dead Dallas a child is lured by the harridan unrelated Hera alongside with the actual-made-imaginative megalithic chamber tomb an action for Dallas as gladiator butt tadpole-like not ever having wept (now she has not wept ever whereas before she did) has been put into this pool the harridan would say from *our* deep inferiority to swim flitting between the condyloma gliding crocodiles that cone-nose skid for this woman's emotion skid unconcerned the crural broken dragging of an injured crummie some crummies grazing crazing the cromorne its cylindrical tube sounds.

Above in the blue the now blank space
shining where the nighthawk was
is open on Dallas.

## Seam

When the child-soldiers have fled Dallas wraps blood-spouting dogsbody in a tourniquet the smallest boy folded into the crocodile hide that she pulls as pulling a sled with dogsbody inside she travels in spring nursing him. She enters the orphaned girls' capital when entry is a cakewalk celebratory ones majestic on floats or horses carry the girls horses are stands for them on floats alongside ones who cakewalk and eat the cakes afterward flock to the living dogsbody loving the small boy at once.

Above in the blue the nighthawk doesn't seize Dallas at the edge of the pool. where she's asleep after. the Antillean doesn't retrieve her for the Mrs.

## Cromorne

As looking into the mirroring pool the powder monkey boy jockey who'd jumped from the race horse's back he'd ridden Amor Asteroid on the plain the horse having wandered back returned from the rhinosporidium but the boy'd seen the reflection of the girl Dallas struggling in the water he reaches in pulling her to the edge of the grassy plain. Draws her to the edge where she lies sleeping. the harridan Hera closes with Herakles grappling. The little girls crying catch the Antillean nighthawk pulling it down from the sky plucking torture it, killing since they've suffered.

# Parachronism

The cricetid pneumotropic clinging at that place (at the lung) on the corpse corpses flung on trash heaps the bud breathing in some of them still flicker in some seaming corpse—Venus arising the arms raised above the ocean of on-lookers with the WHOK! in the air shouting cremorne cylindrical tube's sound a soundless butterfly (the air that the cremorne's sound parted) frenulum a strong spine on the hind wing of the butterfly projecting beneath the forewing serves holds the 2 wings together in flight dives who's Venus WHAP! rallies with such strength the Antillean night-hawk hologram arises 'then'

# Parachronism sieges

Playing is also memory of the present leading to the simultaneous present. Here is up next to it though there are the dead. From the start the present is outside. Watch Venus planet is in present in the children's capital taught by Dallas alongside Des Moines dogsbody and the others the floating horses seen when she'd stared down into the glass percolator that seen in her present dreams now stagger stamping on the floats of the capital she's renamed by the other girls for hearing constant sieges

dictated by the douroucouli tiny night monkey she keeps at her ear the girl not confused clear in these conflicting languages even or especially when she'd weep for the fierce beloved dead Antillean nighthawk "the Kyprian" death and undestroyable wailing with pain with sorrow with rage with fear capable of deep love saturates thought she's breath she goes into the swimming fish the girls called both Venus planet also it is actually the nighthawk that plays as Venus the woman half nighthawk planet "the Kyprian" crossed listening deciphers as 'reads' in the center they listen to this sole bliss-giving judge going to ground when she's hearing everything the man same boy now listening asleep beside her as leaf to stem who is now a man now the powder monkey on the trembling horse at the track where near-by they live as they'd "lived" in the trees.

## Dallas at the front

Dallas now shoved by harridan of decrying megalithic chamber tomb into the deep pool with the crocodiles that twist splashing in turmoil to catch her their huge jaws clash speed together locking them/balled crocodiles in the water—crocodile file of children on the sidewalk reaches the crosswalk—carefully wrapping the dogsbody folded in skin Dallas drags this makeshift sled with him in it rides later bareback dogsbody strapped behind her on the horse she leads the girls lines of them skirting by cities of millions seen far away; many girls die on the way and are buried in the grasslands they run from the flaming burs catching afire as the lines of girls break running amidst the fiery burs they're surrounded by the zooming gazelle-dihedrals shielding them in the aurora borealis the big dipper all the little ones died except those tied several to a horse ten or eleven-year-olds leading walking with Dallas at the front in the mountains the fish that had never seen people jump into their hands where emaciated now they wade to catch food in the clear cold streams near where the Cerynean stag is first sighted Dallas leads them to the capital

# Cromorne

The conchy [conscientious objector] kidnapped forced as a child-soldier to acts lopping with a machete severed the arm of dogsbody the smallest boy, good at seatwork in school but kidnapped is the dustbin drudge 4 the child-soldiers. Yet the conchy after, he's thus fateless—is the dogsbody's invisible missing limb in present moving before him in space where dogsbody dolphin feels his the unseen arm's pleasure boundless though rooted in the bounds as periphery of the/his endless brain? That is the blossom also the same spine's blossom huge? A man believing he was criticizing said "You'd have to *think* about this"—the conchy moves as mind now to where the invisible missing present limb dogsbody's is in future-space a WHOK! is in (not that it's '*in*'?) the bright light-filtering red-dark tree-vaulted leaves fall elating WHOK! in fall's freezing air its sound is not where separate from hearing Venus comes pummeling. 'then' after her is WHOK! as if *hanging* in the air a ring sparkling dully empty hollow in the wake of the air in whose wake its end she lights the court exploding back and forth WHOK! WHOK! 'then' WHOK! 'when' comes apart is beside bright cold the dark-red leaves depart from the elating vault a filter and as if there were no wind a man walks through the red leaves too the full trees' leaves plastered on the walk beneath him that fall bright-dark red hearing everywhere the turning empty driving a dive suddenly freezes returns 2 in the freeze's stop return before 'then' is the rush on the court why isn't it heard elsewhere the grazing herd? With mine waking beside it breaks into its stream. Who'd been the powder monkey on horse shivering dancing racing at the slaver's track the young man at present stands at the fence seeing fierce, loving gaze of Antillean nighthawk the young Venus hover float after hearing WHOK! WHOK! their hearing that's in no space by Venus' invisible limb. 'when.' Ahead, she plays. In women, there are girls—someone makes the open blossom go to its bud backwards. The back (one's spine) is only in elation. Standing in time (sees) Venus. the girl named that ranging among birds wailing with pain rage loose restedness too cuts to pieces.

## Art Credits

*Front cover:* Jess (Jess Collins). *Hera Closing With Herakles*, 1960. Collage, 19.5 x 23.5 inches. Courtesy Tibor de Nagy Gallery, New York. © The Jess Collins Trust.

*pages 10, 119:* Jess (Jess Collins). *Midday Forfit: Feignting Spell II*, 1971. Collage, 50 x 70 x 1.75 inches. Museum of Contemporary Art, Chicago. Photography © Museum of Contemporary Art, Chicago

*page 15:* Masami Teraoka. *Sarah and Octopus/Seventh Heaven*, 2001. Woodblock print, edition of 200, 10.375 x 15.625 inches. Image courtesy of the artist and Catharine Clark Gallery, San Francisco, CA.

*page 18:* Margaret Hofbeck. *Friesian*. Photograph © Margaret Hoffbeck.

*page 33:* Jess (Jess Collins). *The Chariot: Tarot VII*, 1962. Collage, 51 x 33 inches. Courtesy Tibor de Nagy Gallery, New York. © The Jess Collins Trust.

*page 55:* Kiki Smith. *Spinster Series IV*, 2002. Two plate, double printed iris 20 x 14.625 inches, edition of 24. Photograph courtesy of Pace Editions, Inc., New York. © Kiki Smith.

*page 59:* Kiki Smith. *Spinster Series I*, 2002. Two plate, double printed iris, 20 x 14.625 inches, edition of 24. Photograph courtesy of Pace Editions, Inc., New York. © Kiki Smith.

*page 63:* Jess (Jess Collins). *Arkadia's Last Resort: Or Fête Champêtre Up Mnemosyne Creek [Autumn]*, 1976. Collage, 47 x 71 inches. Collection Dallas Museum of Art, General Acquisitions Fund, Dallas.

*page 77:* Jess (Jess Collins). *And A Turtle In A Tree*, 1982. Collage, 20 x 24 inches. Collection Stephens Inc., Little Rock, Arkansas.

*pages 83, 101:* Jess (Jess Collins). *The Unentitled Graces*, 1978. Paper Collage, framed: 41.25 x 61.25 x 3.125 inches. Collection Albright-Knox Art Gallery, Gift of Mr. and Mrs. Armand J. Castellani, 1992, Buffalo, New York.

*page 89:* Kiki Smith. *Spinster Series VIII*, 2002. Two plate, double printed iris, 20 x 14.625 inches, edition of 24. Photograph courtesy Pace Editions, Inc., New York. © Kiki Smith.

*page 106:* Kiki Smith. *Spinster Series VI*, 2002. Two plate, double printed iris, 20 x 14.625 inches, edition of 24. Photograph courtesy Pace Editions, Inc., New York. © Kiki Smith.

*page 115:* Kiki Smith. *Spinster Series V*, 2002. Two plate, double printed iris, 20 x 14.625 inches, edition of 24. Photograph courtesy Pace Editions, Inc., New York. © Kiki Smith.

*page 127:* Jess (Jess Collins). *Hera Closing With Herakles*, 1960. Collage, 19.5 x 23.5 inches. Courtesy Tibor de Nagy Gallery, New York. © The Jess Collins Trust.

## About the Author

Leslie Scalapino (July 25, 1944–May 28, 2010) was born in Santa Barbara, California and raised in Berkeley. She traveled throughout her youth and adulthood to Asia, Africa and Europe—including Tibet, Bhutan, Japan, India, Mongolia, Yemen, Libya, and elsewhere—and her writing was intensely influenced by these experiences. She published her first book, O *and other poems*, in 1976. In 1986, she founded O Books, dedicated to publishing innovative works by young and emerging poets, as well as prominent and established writers. She also taught writing for nearly 25 years at various institutions, including Bard College (16 years in the MFA program), Mills College, the San Francisco Art Institute, and the California College of Arts in San Francisco. She lived with Tom White, her husband and friend of 35 years, in Oakland, California.

Scalapino is the author of thirty books of poetry, prose, inter-genre-fiction, plays, and essays. Recent works include *Flow-Winged Crocodile* and *A Pair / Actions Are Erased / Appear* (Chax Press), two plays published in one volume, *The Animal is in the World Like Water in Water* (Granary Books), a collaboration between Scalapino and artist Kiki Smith, and *Floats Horse-Floats or Horse-Flows* (Starcherone Books), which is a preceding volume to *The Dihedrons Gazelle-Dihedrals Zoom*. Scalapino's *It's go in horizontal/Selected Poems, 1974–2006* was published by University of California Press in 2008. Other books of Scalapino's poetry include *Day Ocean State of Stars' Night* (Green Integer), a collection of eight years of writing; *Zither & Autobiography* (Wesleyan University Press), *The Tango* (Granary Press), a collaboration with artist Marina Adams, *Orchid Jetsam* (Tuumba), *Dahlia's Iris—Secret Autobiography and Fiction* (FC2 Publishers); a reprint of the prose work *Defoe* by Green Integer; and *It's go in/quiet illumined grass/land* (The Post-Apollo Press). A revised and expanded version of her essay book *How Phenomena Appear to Unfold* (originally published by Potes & Poets) is forthcoming from Litmus Press in late 2010.

©Tom White